River Whispers

River Whispers

Glynn Marsh Alam

AVOCET PRESS INC

Avocet Press Inc
19 Paul Court
Pearl River, NY 10965
http://www.avocetpress.com
mysteries@avocetpress.com

AVOCET PRESS

Copyright ©2002 by Glynn Marsh Alam

All rights reserved. No part of this book may be reproduced or transmitted in any form or by any means, electronic or mechanical, including photocopying, recording, or by any information storage and retrieval system, without written permission from the author, except for the inclusion of brief quotations in review.
This novel is a work of fiction and each character in it is fictional. No reference to any living person is intended or should be inferred.

Library of Congress Cataloging-in-Publication Data
Alam, Glynn Marsh, 1943-
  River whispers / by Glynn Marsh Alam.
    p. cm.
  ISBN 0-9705049-5-0
  1. Grandmothers—Death—Fiction. 2. Young women—Fiction. 3. Florida—Fiction. 4. Rivers—Fiction. 5. Rowing—Fiction. I. Title.
  PS3551.L213 R48 2002
  813'.54—dc21

            2002001072

Cover Photograph:
  Front - copyright © 2002 Glynn Marsh Alam

Printed in the USA
First Edition

To the memory of Gambuddy Marsh and Grannie Strickland,
neither of whom appear in this book.

I

I rested my chin on the raw edge of the boat where the oar handle gnawed at the green paint. It took me three days to travel the length of St. Margaret's River, between the fork where it goes south and the Gulf of Mexico. I never entered the Gulf, just floated up to the brackish water where manatees don't bother to dodge propellers. I rowed most of the time. The motor seemed a noisy disturbance to my mission. I slept in the boat last night, in an unzipped bag. Things crawled inside with me, but I didn't mind. I have learned to live with this river, to keep perfectly still when a spider stretches its legs across my chest, probably like moving over a continent to him. He isn't a creature that needs killing. If he leans back on his hind legs and exposes a proboscis, I can fold forward and squash him in a body vise. But that never happened. He drifted onto the wooden slat that serves as a boat seat then into a strand of moss that swept the boat. If he came back, he did so while I slept. I lay in a puddle by morning. Rain had pounded this North Florida river where purple hyacinths carpet the clear running water, and anhinga birds perch in dead cypress trees, spreading their black wings to dry like vampires in a take-off pattern. On the fourth day, cloudless and breezeless, a sore bursa throbbed in my shoulder, and my back muscles tore against the spine. The struggle to move the boat hadn't seemed so bad, but my head dizzied when I tried to sit. From my position on my belly, I tipped the urn over for the last time. A few remaining gray-white particles hit the water, disappearing, perhaps dissolving, too small to follow with my eyes. One last ash floated, bobbing away from shore toward the depths of the river. It swayed, nearly jumping from the surface in the wake of a motorboat, then came to the edge of a small eddy. Twirling, it rotated to the center, then disappeared into the abyss, maybe to rest at the bottom in a crop of dark green eel grass. I envied that ash. Eel grass at the bottom of a river made sense. I rested my chin on the boat until it went numb, then I shut my eyes. I wished my entire body numb.

II

"I lived my good days on that river." Grandma Pope's words had crackled through gums raw and ancient, her voice muscles sticking to the sides of her throat. She drew another raspy breath. "I want to spend eternity down there." She turned her head on the hospital pillow already soiled with drool from a mouth she couldn't quite close. Her brain had snapped, given up its ninety-year program drive, shutting down her withered body, organ by organ. We waited. Joe, Grandma's old friend, nearly as old as she, with a leg and arm withered from a brain stroke like Grandma suffered, had become her little boy, his mind operating at half capacity. He often rolled balls down a dirt incline to watch them bounce in the river. He knew more about Grandma than anybody, but that information was no longer retrievable. Grandma Pope's neck bones cracked as she turned again in the silent room. She stared up from her bed, her rheumy eyes blinking, then focusing, then blinking again, like some far-off signal dying out as the starship enters deep space. "Mae, put me back there."

I pushed forward until my thighs touched her bed, where the odor of rubbing alcohol, lip mint, and fading carnations doused me with impending death. Leaning over, I locked on to Grandma's pupils. She didn't blink. Only the reflection of fright signaled she was still with me. "I promise," I said.

The fright faded. A sound rose from her throat and her life force gave up its shell.

"What's that man doing here?" Aunt Becky's snaky whisper hit my ear like a hot sirocco. I winced, dabbed my eyes and tried to see.

"Who is he?" I leaned across Joe who sat on my left, his tight suit and slicked hair reflecting another era. He stared straight ahead as though he knew Grandma was gone somewhere. He hadn't cried yet.

"One of the Gruman men." Aunt Becky reached for Uncle Nast's arm. She nodded toward the unfortunate Gruman. Uncle Nast gave up emotion long ago. His eyes peered through layers of skin folds at the pew across the aisle and behind us.

"Who are the Gruman's?" A childhood name buzzed around my head like an elusive mosquito.

Uncle Nast's eye folds rested too long on me. The same expression his brother, my daddy, might have used when he wanted me to know this was nothing to ask adults about. Aunt Becky saw it, too, and twitched in her black dress with a lining that rasped across cheap pantyhose. She turned her gaze to the preacher.

Grandma Pope didn't attend her own funeral intact. Her old Primitive Baptist preacher didn't like it much, saying cremation was like dying twice, that he didn't quite know how she could rise on Judgment Day from mere ashes. In a church that washed its congregations' feet and used voices for music, it made no sense to have the body absent, nor in unrecognizable form. Preacher James led the singing, then said some old words in favor of his long-time friend, calling her a "daughter of the river," "a solid righteous Christian," and something of a "justice maker."

He gazed at Mr. Gruman for a long second when he said that. Whispering mosquitoes sounded in my head again. "Now, her lovely granddaughter, Miss Maebell Pope, another daughter of the river, is going to return this brave woman to the place she loved." The preacher nodded toward me, my cue to gently push Joe aside and go to the front. A horse-shoe wreath of carnations and river hyacinths surrounded a bronze-colored urn, what was left of Grandma Pope. I leaned forward, grasped the cool metal in both hands and held it against my chest. The preacher said one last prayer, then touched my shoulder.

I went back to Old Joe who wept now. Somewhere in the depths of his brain, a few synapses had come together with the message that Grandma Pope wouldn't be coming back, that she might even be in this metal jar. He swiped his wet eyes, then touched the urn, leaving a streak of tear across the surface.

Outside, the mosquitoes swarmed. Every once in a while, the name Gruman buzzed. I took my place beside the preacher and waited for the line of condolences. Uncle Nast stared at the circle of women, his wife nearly pawing the earth to be with them, while Grandma Pope rested in her urn behind me on the brick step. Joe drifted off toward the swamp.

"You're not really going down the river by yourself, Miss Mae?" The question followed every "so sorry" I got. I nodded, then looked to the next mourner. Quick hugs and pats on my hand, then necks stretched and eyes turned to catch a look at the dented Ford truck at the edge of the trees.

Mr. Gruman leaned against a fender, sucking a cigar. His belly hung loose over his belt now that he had placed his suit jacket on the hood of the truck. The tie rested there, too. Gruman had almost no hair, and his scalp looked raw from hours in the sun. His face, scratched and rugged, appeared as though he had scraped beard from his face with a flint rock.

"Why is everyone looking at that man?" I said it loud this time, and the mosquitoes scattered.

One sharp-nosed woman with gray sprackled red hair, leaned close enough to my touch my cheek with her lips. "He's not from a nice family." Then she pecked me with a kiss and scurried to join the swarm.

"Well, if he came to my grandma's funeral, he can't be all that bad." I wiped the spot where the woman's lips had left a dab of spit.

"Watch your talk, girl." Uncle Nast finally spoke, his mouth moving between hound-like jowls that drooped along with his happiness.

III

"It's just not a lady thing to do," said Aunt Becky. She agreed to bake greasy, iron-skillet cornbread for my trip. "Out there on that river. Them men, you know, the swamp rats that fish out there all the time. It's not safe, Mae. I mean, what if you're sleeping and one comes along, all drunk and hot up for female... well, you know, don't you?"

I knew. Rape. The old bugaboo, the fate feared for good daughters, a true Southern nasty. It happened more often in colleges and on car dates, but Aunt Becky was sure it would happen to a woman alone on the river.

"Your Uncle Nast is against this." She wrapped the squares of cornbread in foil. "He says you ought to carry a gun."

"No gun. I've got pepper spray, a knife, and the oars can bash a snake." I smiled. "Do you know what a hard oar can do to a man's crotch?"

"Such talk." Aunt Becky turned her back on me. She cut slices of ham, stacked them in plastic containers, then dabbed cranberry sauce in the corners. "Tell your uncle to get the cooler. And deliver this pound cake to Miz Stasia."

"Four days, three nights. Too long for a young woman to be out on that river alone." Uncle Nast helped me push off, his comment directed more to some morality god on a lily pad than to me. "Grandma Pope rowed up and down this river all her life," I said and blew him a kiss. I shoved off to the deep part.

Before I started the motor, I heard his old man's rumble, "Just like her." I had been too long in a state office, the surreal world of sitting on a swivel chair and glossing my eyeballs with computer rays.

The state of Florida will last forever. Nothing will topple the hill upon hill of ants who dart about each other all in the name of exchanging this piece of paper for that one. My river welcomed me. It gurgled at the edges, hummed with giant horseflies, and lapped gently against my boat as though saying, "hello, hello." I passed the fork where the Calico branched away from the St. Margaret. Rounding a curve of overhanging oaks, their moss strands dipping in and out of the water like bathing naiads, I spied a vast grove of purple water hyacinths. I shut the motor and rowed to the edge of the green bulbs. I could have shoved into the mass, disturbed the surface serenity. No grave flowers could match this, and I reached to the back of the boat for Grandma. "First day, first part," I said as I removed the top, then gently shook out a third of the ash. Most of it went under the bulbs and flowers. A little sat atop, making gray spots on noble purple. I replaced the lid when I heard a rustling. A massive, bumpy-hide alligator came down the embankment a few feet away, its body lazily making for the cool water. I watched it pause then open its mouth. Miniatures of the big gator darted about in the water, their short tails flashing back and forth, their bulge-eyed heads straight above the surface.

"Little Miss Alligator, now she had the spirit from the beginning. Wouldn't ride in her Momma's mouth from the nest to the water. No, ma'am! She just jumped outa that egg, through that grass and into the water. Got herself all wet 'fore her brothers and sisters even knew they was supposed to." Grandma Pope sipped from the Mason jar. I had one, too, but my weak lemon tea had grown hot and we were out of ice. Grandma's tea looked dark, like she left the leaves in too long and never put in lemon at all. *"Little Miss Alligator got into that water and found out just who weren't no good down there. Yes, ma'am. She did that little high-pitched croaking kind of sound when her momma got there with the brothers and sisters. She was warning them about what she already seen in that water. And above it, too. Eagle bird just waitin' to have him fresh, tender gator baby for dinner. Moccasin been slithering about some, too. But, Little Miss Alligator, she were born smart."*

Grandma mesmerized me on Sunday afternoons. We had Sunday dinner, then Uncle Nast liked to take a nap. Grandma and Joe sat on the porch with their Mason jars, rocked and refilled the jars. Grandma always said their tea made Joe fall fast asleep and snore in the porch swing. She'd lean back, so far back I though she'd tip over the chair, and gaze up at the beams on the porch. "Dirt dobbers been busy up there. Few spiders, too." Then she'd look off toward the river. "Little Miss Alligator probably got her a bass by this time of day." Every Sunday Little Miss Alligator did something different, like guide to safety the poor little girl who got lost in a rowboat or nudge a swimmer out of dangerous territory.

I guided the boat closer to some cypress trees where debris had gathered to make a straw-colored blanket over the water. The baby gators use this to sit atop in safety, not far from refuge in deep water. In the depths, Momma Gators stand guard, attacking anything that dares disturb their reptilian nursery. One cry from a baby, and a bite might be taken out the side of my boat. I pushed away, turning once to see the purple shine on the river and say goodbye to part of Grandma. Behind me, loud female voices sang "rollin' on the river," and laughed as they canoed in swift unison with their notes, unaware that death had just been celebrated. I waited for the two canoes of five women to pass. They never stopped singing but smiled and waved at me. Their voices faded around the bend, leaving only the echo of their sixties' past. I let my boat bump against cypress knees that grew out of the water almost as though they wanted to tramp to shore. Leaning back, I felt the hot sun on my feet, my face cool in the shade. The women's song left another in my head and it grew louder as I watched the psychedelic sun dart between the branches.

"Blessed Jesus, take me home." Grandma's voice, strong and low pitched, was supported by Joe's tenor. Rocking on her porch, she faced the river. When she sang, folks could ride by in their boats and join in. Joe preferred the porch swing. His back and forth timed his rhythm. On the steps, in my little girl twang, I tried to keep up, but the sound, too glorious to disturb, halted me. While Grandma and Joe drank from their Mason jars, the singing grew louder and more passionate. When Joe leaned over on his chest and fell asleep, Grandma started her stories.

"Tell me about my grandpa," I said once. It hadn't been a good question.

"Your grandpa," said Grandma as she placed the Mason jar in her lap, "been dead for years. I don't remember him." She looked over at Joe who snored as his legs gently moved the porch swing. "Hear that, Old Joe?" She laughed privately. I hushed. "Little Miss Alligator done growed up some. You know that Mae?" She swigged long, emptying the jar.

"When?"

"'tween last story and this one."

"Is she married and having babies yet?" Grandma stared at me. Her eyes, cold and hard, fixed me to the wooden step. I thought my legs would never move again.

"What you know 'bout having babies, girl?" She held the Mason jar by the mouth.

"I just asked…" Grandma never gave me another chance. Grabbing the broom that rested against the wall, she slapped me in the head. Sharp reeds cut into my cheek. I felt one enter my eye as I fell to the next step.

"Don't you go talking 'bout babies!"

And just as quick as the temper hit, it faded. Grandma leaned back in her rocker and hummed. She took no notice of my silent sobs. "Little Miss Alligator decided one day to go exploring up on shore. Her momma been resting in the sun. Told the little lady to stay put near the water, but that girl was sassy. Didn't behave, and was a mite curious, too. She takes off up the bank and runs smack into the longest, ugliest snake you ever did see."

I gasped and dried my tears on my shirt tail. Running into a snake had to be the worst misadventure ever for a person.

"That old snake, he smiled at Missy's face, told her to follow him and he'd show her things she never knew about. Being curious like she was, Missy wagged that green tail and followed the old snake into the swamp. They got to a bunch of rotting logs. Mr. Snake crawled over one and told Missy to follow him. When she reached the top, all she could see was snake, and more snake. That slimy old thing had invited his buddies. They grinned and licked at her with their black tongues. And that first old snake nearly bit Missy's neck. But she was too fast for him. She flew off that log and raced back to her momma, old snakes right behind her. Of course when they saw Momma Gator, they kind of trailed off in different directions." Grandma pressed her lips together. *The humidity wrapped us in steamy heat, but I didn't think the drops coming down her cheeks were sweat.*

My feet grew burny and damp in the swamp boots I wore. I shoved them off and let my bare toes soak up the cool river breeze. Shoving an oar against a cypress knee, I rowed down the river. I sang a grandma song, a hymn she whimpered in the early

Sunday mornings when she pulled the gown over her head and her shoulder ached. I came to her on Sundays, to journey down river to the old church, Joe pushing the oars in his blue boat. Grandma Pope stood tall in church, even when the whispers came strong. Sometimes Joe held my hand and winked down at me. I just sang louder, like Grandma. I knew about whispers. Silly Cathy Cording hated me at grammar school. Her braided black hair and long lashes gave her the right, I guess. In hushed voices I saw them, Cathy and the others down near the tether balls, glimpsing my way and sniggering. Until I decked her, tripped her in a puddle. She ended up skinning that pretty face on the asphalt.

"Please, Grandma, Uncle Nast said it would be okay." I folded my hands in front of Grandma like she was the Virgin Mary. Going on a hayride at thirteen asked for all kinds of trouble, she said. "Boys about that age and a little older interested mostly in exploring."

I wanted to explore, too, but I dared not tell her that. Instead, I praised the idea that it was a church-sponsored outing, that we planned to eat popcorn balls and roast marshmallows over a bonfire when we got to the clearing in the woods. She relented. I joined Cathy Cording and some other silly girls, who paired up with panting boys with greasy hair and bumpy faces, on the back of a truck whose cab had high fences.

Normally, it was used to haul hogs to market, but tonight we filled it with hay and climbed on top. Midwinter, we dragged blankets in with us, and that was Grandma's objection. From some instinct she knew what could happen on a cold night in the dark under a blanket. I watched Cathy Cording flirt with a red-haired boy I'd seen at school. He didn't go to our church and he seemed to be wise about how to put his arm around Cathy's waist and pull her backside flush up against his front. Ten minutes into the ride, she and the redhead cloaked themselves, head and all, under the blanket. From their outline, I could see two bodies press against each other. One boy, whose quest for puberty had not yet been realized, teased them and jerked the blanket from their faces. The redhead's tongue was completely down Cathy's throat! When the cold air hit, he raised his head, and I watched their saliva pull apart like dirty taffy.

Later, on the way back, another boy—I don't remember his name—pulled me under a blanket with him. I tried to forget the saliva and concentrate on his cold lips pressing into mine. I didn't open my mouth, but he didn't either. He pushed hard; I could feel my teeth making marks on the backs of my lips. Once in a while I could feel his spit on the edges of my mouth, drying in the crispy weather. He kept this up until I pushed him away. Sitting up, I let the cold swamp air fill my lungs. I rode all the way back like this, the only body visible above the blankets.

Grandma's song became a choir over the river in the afternoon. Joe said she could convert the bumble bees with that voice. She used gulps from the Mason jar between verses to give her the voice to bellow, "This is my story, this is my song…"

Thunder clapped like an angel telling Grandma to shut up. Clouds arrived overhead. I dreaded this part. In a few minutes I would see lightning hurling from that heaven Grandma sang about. Putting in at Fish Hut Landing, I saw six of them under the tarped structure. Six and one young boy. His eyes widened every time they passed the bottle to him.

The men, guns balancing against the poles, laughed at stories they told each other, getting louder, like Grandma, with each swig. The boy gulped the stuff, too, laughing at his own choking. His jaw went slack when he passed it on, and he grunted as he watched each man gulp down the bitter liquid. It wouldn't do for me to join the swamp rats. I had to look for shelter somewhere else.

Fish Hut Landing used to be the place where river people brought their catch and scaled and gutted it on tables. Inside the huts, they salted it and wrapped it in paper to travel on down the river. The huts were no more than rotted shells now. In the gutting area, somebody had thrown blue plastic over the poles. Up the bank, past the men, I saw a hut with a partial tin roof. I pushed the boat into a grove of water grass between two cypress trees.

Covering my goods and Grandma with my own tarp, I eased onto shore and stalked upward through trees, mud, and brambles. The rain and thunder drowned my noise. Inside the hut, a broken frame of gray wood and rusted tin, I chose a dry spot and slid to the earth. My eyes adjusted to the dimness and I saw a possum raise his front claws at me. I jumped up and kicked at him with my bare foot. He opened his mouth as though hissing, but I couldn't hear it. I kicked again. He turned and scooted into the downpour.

I sat until the rain came through the gapped boards and began to trickle under my toes. I could feel the wetness seep through my pants and tickle my skin. I stood and would have moved to a better spot, but over the pounding rain, I heard a voice like a wounded bird. "Let's go in here, boy."

The Gruman man from Grandma's funeral had hold of the kid's shirt at the neck. "I don't want to," the boy pleaded, struggling to free himself.

"You right for it, kid." Gruman pushed the boy to his knees, stood behind him, and groped at his jeans.

"Wait! Let me." The boy rested his upper body on one shoulder. With both hands he slid down his pants. They floated in muddy water where he had planted his knees. I slipped into a shadow in the corner and prayed for the rain to pound hard for a long time. Gruman shoved his own pants to the ground and bent over the kid. There was no sound, like a video with the mute on. The kid's face twisted and opened as though his skin would stretch into a monster. Gruman's eyes went wild and his body pushed hard against the boy. When it seemed the veins in his neck would pop, he eased back and closed his eyes. The kid sank belly down into the mud.

They didn't stay. Gruman laughed, shut his pants, and ran into the rain. The boy slowly raised himself, sitting bare-butt in the puddle of water. Maybe he cried, but the roof leaked steadily over him. When the lightning moved to the next county, the rain turned to dribble. I could again hear the men down close to the bank. They would be full of liquor by now, the whiskey bottle their war pipe.

I slipped to the door and peered in their direction. The boy loaded guns and coolers into their boats, his jaw slack, his eyes hollow and afraid. The others laughed and hollered orders at him. Gruman peed in the river.

I stayed until my toes coated over with dried mud and my skin itched. The men, down the river somewhere, left a presence of demons, and I thought about Aunt Becky. Like a swamp Indian, I sneaked back to my boat. Checking under the tarp, I sensed Grandma in her urn. "Not here, Grandma. Not where the dirty man peed."

Steam rose from the cool river into the muggy air of an after-rain. My hair, damp from the downpour, turned to glue against my skin. My feet, still coated with dry mud, itched as though I had a fungus.

"Little Miss Alligator stepped in a patch of nettles without her gator-skin shoes," Grandma poked at her battered toes. She leaned over in the porch rocker with an oak seedling branch, stripped of its new leaves, and dug between each toe. Her nails hopped up here and there like yellow mountain ranges. I had seen her take a carpenter's file to the big ones. Flat and cal-

loused, her feet appeared sunburned and peeling, especially around the toes. She dug and dug with the branch. "Oh, that's a good feeling." Then, she'd stop, saying they'd be raw in a minute.

"What did Little Miss Alligator do to her fungus?" I asked, more concerned with the story than Grandma's pleasure in pain.

She turned her eyes to me without moving her head. "She got it on somebody," she laughed. "You look girl," she pointed to her own toes. "If I was to rub my foot on yours, you'd catch it and be rubbin' with a stick, too."

I recoiled and shoved my little butt across the steps.

"Now, Little Miss Alligator, she got the stuff when she went into the woods and saw something. Came upon this big old bull gator some say went mad when a poacher hit him with a baseball bat but didn't kill him. Old Bull done caught one of Little Miss' sisters—from a later batch of eggs— and tried to crush her in the mud. Little Miss wasn't having none of that. She up and popped the old bull with a canoe oar she'd found on the side of the river. Shoved the old bull off her sister over on his back. Now," Grandma's eyes widened as she leaned toward me, "everybody knows no gator can do much on his back. Old Bull lay there with his mouth open but didn't make a sound. Little Miss prodded her sister and told her to run." Grandma leaned back in the rocker, her lips pursed in triumph. "Little Miss saved that sister, yes sir!" She suddenly leaned over and attacked an especially bad itch. "But got the toe fungus to remember it by!"

I sat on the river, far enough from shore to avoid grass critters, but not in the swift currents yet. My toes itched. I ducked both feet into the cool water and swished off the mud. Propping my legs on the edge of the boat, I let them dry in the sun. The longer I sat, the farther the swamp rats would be from me. Listening in the quiet, I could hear the undercurrents, the spring water that shot from a deep limestone cave into the big river, laced itself through waving green eel grass, then gathered momentum as it headed to the Gulf. Like lemmings, I thought, headed over the cliff. I wondered if I hitched myself to a current would it take me to the Gulf, through brackish water, finally to a salty storm of waves that housed crabs and sharks.

I had swum once near one the limestone caves, the massive one where they found a mastodon skeleton. Frigid water races from that big door to the depths, enough to furnish a nearby resort hotel. Far below, I gazed at huge catfish who cleaned the white sides of the river and the cave. Tiny fish frolicked down there, too, hanging around petrified tree limbs that fell when the Indians worshiped these waters. No place for Little Miss Alligator, I thought. No gator ventures that deep.

"Doesn't take much water to drown something," I said aloud, and a crane stood at attention until I passed it and made for an overhang. When fear gave over to hunger, I paddled the boat under an oak grove. The trees grew on the shore but had bowed to the river years ago. Coolness surrounded me.

Shoving Grandma to the very end of the boat, I pulled the small cooler toward me. Packed ice, then cornbread, sliced ham, a tomato, and tea, filled me with the familiarity of Aunt Becky. I liked eating outdoors, after a rigorous rowing. It made me hungry, reminded me of the strength of Southern sustenance. I stayed long in the grove, moving out only when I saw a copperhead venture onto one of the overhanging branches. I followed him with my eyes until he disappeared into a clump of moss, invisible but dangerous. Late afternoon shadows cooled the steam on the river. I hadn't used the motor yet. At one shady spot, where the wide river lane narrowed where long branches reached from shore, I stopped to watch an ancient fisherman check his bush hooks, lines hung from overhangs to snare catfish. He had marked his lines with yellow ribbons tied to tree branches. There were others, red and green and pink, scattered nearby, like territorial markers of a food source.

The man spat brown snuff into the water, then raised himself on bowed legs. He stood for a shaky moment until the boat stilled itself. Gnarled fingers gently lifted a line. At the end, a long-whiskered catfish flapped against death as he heaved it into his boat.

Pulling on the tree branch, he slid the boat a few feet forward and grabbed hold of another line. This time, the fish danced furiously in the air. The old man pulled up to free it from the hook, then caught my stare. Familiarity struck me, something around his eyes and maybe the smirking mouth full of snuff.

He stared the Gruman stare and must have sensed my fear for he loosened his grip on the fish just as its mouth broke from the hook. The fish leaped hard into the air, out of the man's hand, and dove into safe depths. The man cursed, but I couldn't hear his words. With one hand still holding the empty line, he raised a fist into the air. "Lucky fish," I whispered. "Swim far and don't come back."

IV

"You messin' with my lines, woman?" The voice shouted over years of built-up tobacco smoke, its growly rasp setting birds flying. He waved a shaky finger toward the end of my boat where one of his yellow ribbons flapped like the birds' wings. Up close, its brightness faded, it was tattered and stained like its owner.

"Not hardly," I called back to him and turned on the motor. I didn't look back, but bumps of fright popped up on my neck. He would find his clan, as sure as a snake sheds, and let them know a lone female was traveling the river.

Aunt Becky's face flashed through the fine mist that hit my face off the wake. "No decent girl is safe out there alone. Get married and find your safety," she'd say as though Uncle Nast's morose solitude would defend her against the Gruman men. Run away, he'd say. Stay away, hide, don't confront. "Don't be Little Miss Alligator," I whispered.

"How'd my daddy and mama go to heaven?" I asked in a rare quiet moment on Grandma's front porch. She had sung her hymns and told her stories. Now, she reposed, staring out at the river, nursing a near empty jar. Without looking at me, she said, "Korea and cancer."

The alliteration hit me, and I repeated it like a mantra.

"You're a lucky orphan. Your Aunt Becky couldn't have no kids. She grabbed you up soon as your mama took ill. Your daddy off in Korea got mighty shook up when he heard his wife wouldn't be around when he got back. Didn't matter much. Koreans shot him up; he never came back."

Silence fell over the porch like I'd never heard before. I slid to the bottom step and wiggled my bare toes in the dirty river sand. Dampness engulfed my foot as I dug deep, and I wondered if my mama could feel it over her body in the grave.

A stray cat moved from under the house, stretching its wormy body and yawning, then darting out to chase a bark-colored lizard through the sparse grass. With my eyes, I followed the chase to the river's edge until I spied a red canoe drifting downstream. Two people, a man and a woman, sat at each end, their heads thrown back, mouths open. The woman, leaning to her left, let her hand drag the water.

"Grandma!" I stood up suddenly.

"Child, don't holler like that." She sat up straight.

Uncle Joe snorted in his sleep. "That lady might get her hand bit off if she hangs it in the water like that."

"What lady?" Grandma stared at the river. The red canoe slowed its drift when it rammed against a heavy bed of hyacinth. I watched Grandma's face. The ruddiness of an afternoon jar turned to bluish pale.

"Joe! Wake up, Joe!" Whispers, and none for my ears, surrounded me all evening and into the dark night when Grandma Pope insisted we stay with her. Uncle Nast said she ought to go home with us, but she'd hear none of it. "Sheriff said to stay put."

Early the next morning, I drank hot chocolate with my grits. I sat at the rough wood table in the kitchen, my feet cold against the sandy linoleum. Across from me, a deputy in uniform—his eyes red and baggy—slurped on his coffee mug. Grandma had two percolators going on the stove, and the smell of coffee grounds permeated the wood-frame house.

"What you think?" said another uniformed deputy who came into the kitchen and poured his own brew.

"Murder-suicide," said the one at the table. "Note found on the man."

"In a canoe?"

The standing deputy dumped a spoon of sugar into the coffee cup. "Didn't want to dirty up the house or the car for their kids. Canoe was rented."

The sitting deputy placed both hands around his mug, and looked up at me. "Little girl, you'd best go play in your room."

I shook my head. "Were they married?"

"Not now, little girl." The sitting deputy scowled at me, then passed his mug to the other man for a refill.

Later, when the deputies had taken away the man and woman and their canoe, I rested my head against Grandma's knees. She liked the twilight on the river. A gentle breeze blew away the humidity, while crickets and frogs harmonized, using the rhythmic squeak of Uncle Joe's swing as a metronome. "You've lived a long time, Grandma," I said.

"Not long enough," she answered.

"I'll never marry, Grandma." I hugged her calves.

"You say that now." She patted my hair.

"I won't. Marriage kills you."

Grandma's hand rested heavy on my head, and she made no sound at all. Then, she shoved me gently away and began to rock, the runners making click-clack on the porch boards. In the distance, I heard a cat, its timed yowls, deep and whiny, calling for a mate.

V

I cut the motor when I came to The Cove. We called it that, even though there had to be many coves on the river. This inlet was where Old Joe stowed his boat all those years he came to see Grandma. Sometimes, we put our own boat there and filled it up with fried chicken, deviled eggs, and cornbread, and hauled it to the church. There, we'd spread it on long wood tables set up on the grounds. People from all around added their greens, biscuits, and baked hams along with banana pudding, pies, and cobblers. Without their Mason jars, Grandma and Old Joe smiled and shook hands. I chased about with the other children, finding hiding places behind fallen tree trunks and palmetto bushes.

With Grandma in one hand, I tossed the rope over a landing pole that still stuck out of the water. Something on the bank moved. I stood perfectly still until a long, pipe-colored water moccasin slid into the river and disappeared under some lily pads. I pushed up over the little hill, then wound through a grove of pines. I stopped. River wind had kicked up and passed through the pine needles, making sounds like humming angels. I felt the cushion of old needles under my feet and smelled the sappy pine rosin. Hugging Grandma close to my chest, I stood still.

"They is places in the woods, child, to hide even the most troubled soul— good and evil alike." Grandma leaned over to snatch up two pine cones and toss them in a paper sack. *"This here's one of them."* She leaned against a pine tree and shut her eyes. *"I come here many times when I was young, you just can't imagine."*

"Did you have a troubled soul then, Grandma?"

Grandma chuckled, then frowned. *"Had one then, sometimes got one now."* She turned to me, eyes flaming. *"And you'll have your own, Mae. Just wait!"* She moved from me, scouring the ground like pine cones were things you couldn't see too well.

It hit me hard, that "troubled soul" stuff. I believed in Jesus like the preacher told me to, even went up during a meeting and took Him personally in front of the congregation. Doing that embarrassed me for weeks, especially with all the grownups telling me how good it was that I did it.

The preacher often talked about troubled souls, people who'd committed murder or thieves who robbed from their neighbors. I'd never done that and didn't plan to. How could I ever have a troubled soul? Maybe it was something you got when you grew up, something everybody had to get then go to the woods to settle.

"Will I get one often?" I tagged after Grandma.

"What?" She stooped over, her face red and determined.

"A troubled soul?"

Grandma stood up to glance over the clearing among the pines. *"What makes you ask that?"*

But it wasn't a question. I knew the tone that drifted off into another thought. It was a nice way of saying shut up.

"Well, Grandma," I said as I sat the urn on a bed of pine needles. "You never did tell me but you were right. I do get a troubled soul at times." I heard a limb crack. My soul lost its troubles, and the instinct to survive took hold. Reaching into my pocket, I withdrew the pepper spray and lifted off the safety. Softly, I drew the urn close to me. A Gruman in these woods would get fire in the face if he came near me.

Somewhere in my head, I heard Aunt Becky say in Grandma's voice, "Silly girl, Gruman's know these woods better than anybody. No little thing of pepper spray will fend them off."

My eyes darted through palmettos, seedlings, and tall pine trunks. When they found four hoofed legs, thin and beige-colored, I sighed relief. I stood, and the deer shot off, leaping like a ballerina through the underbrush. I followed the pine tree growth to the edge of Grandma's homestead. Old Joe would have walked this way from the bank, the route from his cabin on the other side of the river. He came early in the mornings and ate a sliced-white-bread breakfast with Grandma. She'd place a whole loaf in a warm oven, then take it out and rip open the package. Old Joe got out honey and butter and swiped it around in his plate until it was creamy mixed. With a piece of the warm bread, he wiped it up and put the whole thing in his mouth. When I slept over, I ate with him, swiping and stuffing the sweetened bread into my mouth.

"Don't eat so much at one time," Grandma said. "You'll choke yourself."

"But Joe does it that way."

Grandma looked at Old Joe and a glow came over her face. I loved Old Joe for giving her that look. "Joe's a big man, honey. He got more capacity than you."

"Besides," grinned Joe, his sticky bread hanging to one side of his mouth, "you a lady, and ladies just can't eat like this. Won't find no husband that way."

"I ain't looking for one." I stuffed my mouth again.

"One might be looking for you," he said.

"Don't start," said Grandma and patted Joe on the arm. "She'll be after

the boys soon enough."

"Not me." I knew that for a fact, until I thought of Kenneth Buchanan from grammar school. He liked to chase me on the playground, and for some reason, it was more fun than when Shirley Mason did the same thing.

"Plenty boys out there," said Joe. He looked at Grandma and changed the subject.

Later, when Joe helped Grandma in the kitchen, she whispered to him, "I just hope none of them Gruman boys come near our baby."

"They do and you know what I'll do." Joe glanced back my way and winked. "Got to find somebody super special for Mae."

I stood in the sand near the river bank. Grass had grown tall around the old wood and cement blocks that had been Grandma's house. Part of the steps were still there. When I sat on one, it growled and cracked, and flying termites took to the air, sending me straight back up on my feet again. I strolled around for a few minutes, but I couldn't even find where the kitchen or the back porch had been. Like Grandma, the house was crumbles now, replaced by wild swamp grass.

I gazed at the urn, then turned to the river's edge. Pulling open the lid, I began to shuffle a few ashes into the water.

"What you puttin' in that river, girl?" A low voice, like someone who didn't talk much, startled me. Slamming the lid on Grandma, I turned to face a bow-legged, leather-skinned man who might have been ninety. He leaned on a stick, stripped of its leaves.

"Just sending Grandma home," I said and looked around for the man's companions. There weren't any.

"You burn your Grandma?" The man used his free hand to swipe at drool at the corner of his mouth. I could hear the skin of his fingers rasp against the half-shaven face.

"Cremated, yes." A coldness began to move inside me, from my knees to my abdomen. Aunt Becky warned me about this, how strange men lived in the swamp and could sneak up on you just like that.

"Better you get on out of here before nightfall." The man leaned both hands on the stick. Mosquitoes swarmed about his dirty cap. He didn't seem to mind. "Lots of evil doers in these woods."

"Are you alone?"

"For now. What you want to know for?" He drew a black veined hand across his mouth.

"Did you know my Grandma? Pope was her name. She lived up there." I pointed to the barely visible ruins.

"Old Lady Pope? Sure, I knowed her." The man laughed slightly, then stared wide-eyed at me. "How'd she die?"

"Stroke." The man's head bobbed up and down like he approved of that method of death. "Stubborn woman, good though. Take something like that to fell her."

"How well did you know her?"

The old man pulled off the cap and fanned away the mosquitoes. "She were one of my girlfriends 'bout sixty years back." He broke into a gummy grin, then laughed. It came from deep, rising in a dirty joke way, like I used to hear from some of the beer-drinking men who hung around Lakemore's River Store.

"Are you a member of the Gruman family?"

The man stiffened, then began to shake his finger at me. "Not damn hardly! Scum, them people. You best stay away from them."

"Why?"

"Ask your Grandma, right there." He pointed a crooked finger at the urn. "She got her stories about them people."

"Well, sir, Grandma is in no shape to tell me right now. Maybe you could act as a stand-in and tell me yourself. What did you say your name is?"

"Skipper, and that's all you need to know." He eyed me, then slowly lowered his gaze to the urn again. His pupils took on a pitiful glow, one of profound sadness built of harsh days inside this swamp. I wondered if he had set a record for going without human companionship sometime in his history.

"Skipper, this is the last of my grandmother. I'd like to know about her." I tried to plead, to hint at his own few remaining days.

"See that bank there?" His hand trembled as he forced it to rise and point toward the river. "Your grandma shot a gator right through its thorny head one time. She were a young girl then. Had a man working round here, but he were too scared to shoot. That barefoot queen just grabbed the shotgun and blasted the demon right out of that gator. He'd ate a dog of theirs." Skipper added this last information softly, an anticlimax to the shooting.

"And the Gruman family, what about them?"

"Uh-uh," he shook his head. "Bad crop them Grumans. Anybody living in these swamps going to meet up with them sooner or later. Your grandma—lord she were a pretty thing!" He slapped a hip. "She got to courting, and one of the Gruman boys came round to see her. She run him off with that same shotgun. Said she didn't like no boys who run with their sisters." Skipper's saloon laugh sounded again, and his rheumy eyes glowed with pleasure. He reached into his back pocket and pulled out a bottle. "Like some?"

I shook my head, wary of this old man. I could break him in half in no time, but his mind had landed in a permanently dirty spot.

"Run with his sisters?" I knew that meant incest, but Skipper may have been trying to shock me, to make some helpless female dread his masculine threat of rape just one more time before the six-feet-under hit him. He smiled, raised the bottle and forced amber liquid down his wrinkled gullet. Choking, he leaned over, and spit most of the liquor on the ground.

"Sick old man," I said and turned my back on him. I didn't remember seeing this man when I visited Grandma's house. If he was as nasty then as now, she would have run him off, too.

"You be careful now, hear?" He shuffled behind me through pine straw, the brown needles covering his ankles and scratching their way up his pants legs. Once in the boat, I turned back. Lifting the paddle in his direction, I asked, "You know Old Joe?"

"Old Joe? Sure thing. Him and me go fishing round here sometimes. Been doing it since we were boys."

He held up the cane and waved it as I backed away from the bank. I turned again when I picked up the deep river current. He still had the cane in the air. The other hand raised to his eyes, almost like he was wiping tears. "Nasty old man," I whispered to no one.

I traveled this river since I was a toddler, and my first real memory of being with family was sitting in the front of a boat, somebody holding onto me, and the river breeze blowing across my face. A tingling joy rose in me then, and I wanted it back now. I revved up the motor and shot down the center of the river. Cutting the throttle, I paced it slowly. A light spray hit my face. The only person on this part of the river, I should have felt safe, happy like that little kid on the front of the boat. My stomach gnawed and I stopped the motor. The boat drifted, the water lapping at the edges. Grandma, secure in her urn, stared at me from the boat floor, and I envisioned Skipper, bowlegged and swamp odorous, waving his cane at me. Night would arrive and I dreaded it.

I remembered nights camping under the stars with Girl Scouts, then another time with a church group. Preteens who told ghost stories and lighted circular burners to stave off mosquitoes, we hauled our sleeping bags under pup tents. We took turns talking of people who woke in the morning with a rattler curled up at their waists, or of someone who decided to take a tinkle in the woods and never returned. The swamp cooperated and gave us banshee cries and flutters in the underbrush. No one could see beyond the campfire. Even the river water flowed by us, carrying the giant gator who held the missing girl in its jaws. We couldn't see, but surely everything out there could see us. I had to make camp as planned, to once again unfold my sleeping bag and lie on shore. In my grownup head, I knew the rattler wouldn't want me for a bed partner. I wasn't sure about the Grumans.

VI

"Lordy, child, I'm so glad to see you." Grandma enfolded me and gave me the only kiss I ever remember from her. She and Uncle Nast stood on the dock where our counselors deposited us after a three-day outing. Grandma hugged and squeezed, then suddenly let go. *"Get your gear, and let's be off home."*

I looked at Uncle Nast. Even then his face sagged and took on the gray dog look. He winked and rubbed my hair.

"I just was gone three days," I said, guilt covering my little girl psyche.

"And you won't be doing it again," said Grandma. She grabbed my hand and pulled me beside her. Uncle Nast trotted behind us with my duffel bag.

"Now, Ma, she's all right. Don't go gettin' riled up some more." Uncle Nast spoke to her like she might turn round and pop him one.

"What did I do?" I tugged on Grandma's hand and tried to talk sideways to Uncle Nast.

"Nothing, Mae," he said. *"Your Grandma just got worried a little."*

"Such goings on in the woods," said Grandma, and I knew she was working up to something, either spanking me or telling me something awful had happened.

"Is Aunt Becky all right?"

"Fine, Mae, just fine. She's cooking you up some fried oysters right about

now. Not just anybody got the ability to eat oysters, now do they?"

Grandma pushed me into the back seat of the Ford, then crawled into the driver's seat. Uncle Nast put my bag in the trunk and jumped in the passenger side just in time for Grandma to ram the gas pedal hard enough to skid the tires. It doesn't take a child long to blame herself for an atmosphere, and I tore out my insides worrying long before we finished the mile to Grandma's house. Uncle Nast never turned to talk to me from the front seat. He'd glance sideways at Grandma who kept her eyes on the road. Supper of fried oysters, hush puppies and slaw sat on the table in Grandma's linoleum-floored kitchen. Uncle Nast ate two helpings of everything. I nibbled, scrunched in my chair like an elf in a giant's seat. Grandma fidgeted, her eyes watering over. Finally, she got up and went into her bedroom. I heard her mutter something about needing to see Joe.

Later, when Aunt Becky and I had cleaned up the dinner dishes, she told Uncle Nast to go sit on the porch awhile. She and I busied ourselves sweeping up the dead bug rings around the lamps when she decided to talk. "Seems some child got killed on the river last night." She tried to act like it was a newspaper headline from across the world. I stopped to count all my camp friends in my head. "It wasn't an accident, Mae. That's why your grandmother was upset."

"What was it?"

"Well," Aunt Becky frowned and tilted her head like she did when she wanted things to be gentle and knew they really couldn't be. "Seems someone harmed her, enough to kill her."

I knew. Aunt Becky didn't have to say it. We learned things in the scouts, and some of my friends read True Confessions *enough to define the dreaded word, if not the act.*

"Does that kill you?" From the stories I heard it was sure enough painful, especially if he forced you, but I'd never heard of death being associated with it. Maybe it was like getting stabbed.

"Oh, child!" Aunt Becky's eyebrows creased, and I wondered if she were

chastising me for not knowing much or begging not to be asked anymore. "He beat her badly." She said this on inhale, then darted off to get a trash can.

I lay in bed staring up at a yellow leak stain in Grandma's wood ceiling. The stain took on a shape, kind of like a canoe with an Indian face in it— no body, just a face riding inside a canoe. Strangely, I couldn't feel for the little dead girl, couldn't see her battered face and body. She had made Grandma kiss me. Maybe she was embarrassed about it, but she did it anyway. I smiled and turned over for a nice sleep in a real bed.

I didn't want to camp under the stars alone tonight, but I had no choice. Miz Stasia wasn't expecting me until tomorrow night. I rowed until it was too dark to be on the water, then began looking for a clearing near the shore. In the distance, I heard singing. On the bank near a deer run, a campfire burned between two tents. Two canoes rested beside a clump of palmettos. One woman played a guitar while the others harmonized "morning is breaking," and passed each other a lone cigarette. I edged the boat closer. "Come on up," yelled a woman as tall as Old Joe, bone-thin with a long gray braid down her back. They all stood, except the one with the guitar, and watched as the thin one met me at shore. "You alone on the river?"

I nodded and let her tie my boat to a tree branch.

"I'm Lillian Street," she said and stuck out a strong hand. "These are my friends from a long time ago."

"Mae Pope." I shook her hand and surveyed the bevy of women. There were five counting Lillian, and all in their fifties, it seemed. "Are you camping here?"

"Been doing for about five years now," said Lillian. She introduced me to the others by first name. "We call ourselves 'The Ageless Hippies.'"

"You're alone? No husbands?" I don't know why I found this strange. I was alone, too, but then I always had been.

"Dead or divorced," said the one called Sylvia who giggled and grabbed the sleeve of a petite Annie. "We like it better this way."

"We don't fit in the sewing or church circles, you see."

Lillian offered me a folding chair, then pulled another one from a van parked behind the tents. "We sit on chairs. Ground sitting stiffens our legs at this age." She chuckled along with the others. "We like this life and decided why not do it once in a while. We know how to do all the outdoor stuff." She smiled broadly and stretched her arms in pride at the tents firmly fastened to the swamp floor.

"You're not afraid of the swamp?"

"What's to fear? A few snakes? Besides, we got protection." Lillian made a gun-like gesture with her thumb and index finger.

"I guess I mean of the humans in the swamp?"

Sylvia giggled again and added, "Like she said, we got protection."

"You live on this river?"

Lillian offered me a soda she pulled from a cooler. I watched my boat bump gently back and forth with the tiny lapping waves. Eel grass stuck its pointy blades up around the bottom every now and then. In the forest that enclosed us, a chorus of frogs sang the approach of night. In the distance, sky hues of dark blue overtook the shades of red sunset. I rested well in the chair. In a few words, I explained my journey. "And it's been a bit scary up to now." I told them of Skipper and the Gruman fisherman. But, the incident in the shed stuck in my throat. I couldn't reveal it.

"Oh, yes, the Gruman family. We know about them, right?"

Lillian looked around at her camping sisters. They nodded.

"Had trouble with a couple of them once," said Sylvia, her eyes wide within the plump cheeks. She wore a vest over a short-sleeved tee, and jeans that nearly dragged the ground. Her oval shape reached from neck to knees. "They came by a couple trips ago. Tried to join us, then threatened to come back in the night."

Annie chimed in, "Lillian and Carrie over there pulled guns right away and ran those two coots off in a second. Never saw them again, but we hear stories every now and then."

Carrie, a big woman whose heavy hips tugged at her slim waist leaned forward. She wore a large diamond engagement ring over a single band. "That family has legends surrounding it, and after meeting those two, I believe them."

"Can you tell me some—of the legends, I mean?"

"Why not. But let's eat first." She offered no invitation, not even a question of whether or not I was hungry. Like an animal pack, they accepted me, pulled me into their circle of safety, and I breathed relief that I would stay the night here. Lillian and Sylvia hauled plastic containers from the van and placed them on unfolded television trays. Carrie and Annie pulled mustard and relish from the cooler, while a tiny quiet woman named Fran opened a brown bag of paper plates and napkins.

"Stoke the fire, will you?" Lillian called to me. I reached for the thick branch and stirred up the flames. We used thin tree limbs, scraped of their leaves, to roast wieners over the open fire. From the plastic case, we fished out buns and filled them with condiments. Annie returned to the van and brought a chocolate cake which she sliced and served along with ice cream from another cooler. A little guilt nagged at me when I thought of Aunt Becky's ham and cornbread waiting in my own cooler, but I wouldn't disturb this scene for all the cornbread in the world.

The stories came slowly, gossip, like we were sitting around a backyard barbecue, and peppered with laughter. I never knew how much of anything could really be true.

"My ex-husband told me those Grumans are all in-bred," said Sylvia, her eyes dancing in the firelight. "Said he once came across them in the little market down near the ocean. I don't mean all of them. Lord knows there must be dozens, but an old man and two young ones, teens, I think. He—my husband—said they had these big old jaws and scraggly hair and some kind of big pop eyes that wouldn't stop staring. The gruff old man had to tell them two kids over and over to pick up this, pick up that, bring it to the counter. Like they were retarded."

"My daddy used to tell stories of how the Gruman's sometimes got themselves killed." Like a grandmother reading to an amazed child, Annie's face smiled and grimaced as she took up the tale. "Said they do it anywhere in the woods, and people have just walked right up on them."

"It?" Lillian smiled.

"Yes, it. Oh, you know what I mean." Annie tapped her hand on her friend's sleeve. "You mean what we used to do in those college communes we lived in back in the sixties?"

Lillian bobbed her head playfully. Sylvia whooped out loud, stood up, then sat back down suddenly. "Can you believe those things we did! We're such prudes now."

"We're grandmothers now, for heaven's sake," said Annie. "We can't do that."

"Can too." Quiet Fran spoke without expression. "I did it just last week." The forest silenced. Even the frogs stopped singing while the other women turned their heads to their camping companion. "Damn nice, too." Fran pulled the wiener from her bun, held it up then took one end into her mouth and sucked in half of it. With an audible chop, she bit it in half.

Swamp silence burst into rolling laughter. Women slid down in their chairs or scrunched up their knees, hollering in glee. All except Fran, who ate the other half of her wiener.

"I heard that a few of the Gruman men have been knocked off over the years."

"And not a few of the Gruman women got knocked up."

"And," Annie leaned forward, "it was the Gruman men that knocked them up!" Again and again they laughed. They seemed easy with each other, eager to express and accept. I wanted to hear more of the Gruman tales, but I didn't want to end the mirth, a sense long buried in my bureaucratic soul.

When the stomach aches from laughing hard got too much, Sylvia said, "Okay, girls, I got to pee! If some damn snake bites my butt, you come running with the kit."

"Just hold on," said Fran who ran into a tent and retrieved a roll of toilet paper. "I got to go, too."

"You can bring up your bag and stay in our tent," said Lillian. "Carrie and I have room."

I walked to my boat, out of the firelight. From the river's edge I could see Lillian douse the fire and the other women put away the food. The tents, their orange canvas looking dark blue in the pale light, stood like fortresses. From the woods, I heard Sylvia laugh at some joke. A clear patch of sand lay near the shore. In the darkness, I shucked my shoes, pulled down my pants and urinated from a squatting position. The warm liquid hit my feet. That meant I'd have river sand stuck between my toes all night. I hadn't done that since my scouting years.

Later, Carrie, the only one who smoked real tobacco, left the tent for open air. Lillian and I sat on our sleeping bags in the dark. "Do any of you really know anything about the Grumans,"

I asked.

"Probably nothing we can prove. I heard a serious conversation once when I was a kid about a Gruman gone missing. The Gruman family wanted to blame somebody for killing him, but the sheriff said he probably drowned. Heard that off and on over lots of years. But, who knows?"

The river waters moved like blood in a giant vein. We sensed its sound more than heard it as we lay in the dark. Within the silence, crickets rubbed their legs together and played their monotonous tune, while frogs bloated their throats and kept a steady beat.

"Oh, hell!" yelled Annie from the other tent. "I can't sleep. Let's sing." And she started on a chorus of "Michael row the boat ashore, hallelujah…"

We joined in, providing harmony, a choir sound from a female sextet. I sang in a breathy alto, and pictured our notes traveling through the forest where Little Miss Alligator sat on a log and tried to snatch the notes into her mouth, maybe to keep them from reaching all the way to the Gruman house.

I lingered in The Ageless Hippies' camp until late morning. They stirred cold cereal with artificial sweetener in plastic bowls, and I provided the one cantaloupe Aunt Becky had stuffed into the cooler. "We plan to canoe all the way to the river fork and have lunch at that hole in the wall," said Sylvia. "We hear it has great catfish."

For a moment, I thought of the bush hook fisherman, probably a Gruman, and wondered if he sold to that cafe. Lillian shook my hand as I untied my boat. "Take care and do your grandma a proper strewing," she said. I shook her hand and nodded, my throat lumpy with gratefulness.

"Listen," she said. "Take my number. Call us if you think you might like to go camping, or join us on any of our little trips into abandonment. We've been known to invade Gulfport to gamble, and we're thinking of Mardi Gras next year."

I took the paper and stuffed it into my jeans pocket. "I will," I said and sat in my boat. I wouldn't use the motor. I wanted to row away slowly.

When I finally rounded the bend in the river, I looked back to see four women high on the bank and one at the river's edge. They raised their hands in unison almost like an invisible, magical connection between angel witches.

VII

Alone again, I drifted, taking up the oars only when the boat threatened to entangle itself in a grove of lily pads. The sun shone hot above me, and not a single breeze blew across the lazy waters. I wanted to sleep, to melt into the wood and let the river float me like a leaf on the currents. Aunt Becky, Uncle Nast, my desk job seemed like life on another planet now. When I lay back, my hair brushed the urn where a direct ray of sunlight reflected energy. I felt what Grandma felt, what she meant when she said to rest her here for eternity.

"You ought to marry, Mae," Aunt Becky put eternal commitment in with the dish water. "You getting on up there, and babies don't come easy with age." She glanced at me, her sorrow at never having a single pregnancy forcing her to look back quickly at the roasting pan she scrubbed with steel wool.

"Babies don't need a wedding, Aunt Becky," I said to disturb her meddling. "Your cousin can tell you."

"Now, listen here, Mae. My cousin made her own...." She started to say bed, but realized the pun and turned back to the sink. Aunt Becky had never lived down her cousin Dorie's transgressions—which is what the church

called them back then. Dorie, just seventeen and not out of high school, suddenly let everyone know she'd be in a wedding in a month—her own. I had never attended a wedding before but I knew you got to wear a white dress, and men took the ladies' arms and seated them in the pews, then everybody went to a hall somewhere and had lots of cake and punch. The big thing, however, was that the bride and groom had to kiss each other in front of the preacher, God, and the entire congregation.

Grandma kept me a whole week while Aunt Becky went to help Dorie and her mom prepare for the big day. I heard a lot of groaning about having to let out the seams in a wedding dress. "Silly girl," Grandma mumbled to herself as she swept sand off the porch. "Done got herself a handful of trouble before she's old enough to know what trouble is."

When I looked up and started to ask, "What trouble?" I got such a scowl that I went back to playing with my pick-up sticks. I pulled out the different-colored thin sticks from a round can, held them in a bunch, then let them fall on the floor. They stacked up in a maze, but I could ease my fingers on the ends and pick them up, one by one, top to bottom. Most of the time, I did them all. But when Grandma swept too hard, complained too loudly, I tangled up my insides like the sticks. Somehow, I could never untangle either of them very well. The joy taken out of the sticks, I retreated to the river bank to deal with my insides.

The day of the wedding, I was knotted up like a fish net in eel grass. My new yellow church dress didn't fit right, but Grandma said no one would notice, that the only dress anyone would stare at would be Dorie's. I sat on the pew next to Grandma. Miz Stasia brought four of her kids and sat behind us. Aunt Becky and Uncle Nast had to sit with Dorie's family. A pinched mouth lady who looked to be skin over skeleton came out and played some music at the organ. When she suddenly burst into the "Wedding March," my guts tumbled.

Dorie's intended came out with another man, both dressed in tight suits. The intended sported a crew cut of light red hair, short enough you couldn't tell if maybe he weren't bald. His face, ruddy and swollen, looked to me like one of the boys in school who got bee bit all over one time. There were no bridesmaids. Grandma said under the circumstances, none were needed.

Dorie came walking up the aisle, her old paw looking stiff in his shiny suit. He had his arm folded for her to hold onto, and his big rough hand stood out against the blue coat. He'd tried to clean his farmer's nails but they still had a line of dirt deep to the cuticle. The skin peeled back in places across his fingers. When I looked at Dorie's intended, his hands looked the same. For a moment, I felt those thorny hands run across my neck. Dorie's entrance set the eyes to wagging, since the tongues had to be quiet in church.

The wedding dress, a long thing of satin and lace, had no shape. Her middle was as big as her bust and hips. The new, so-called "sack" dress was all the rage at the time; I figured Dorie had bought one to keep in style. Since grown-up women never approved of the new styles, I didn't wonder at the suspecting glances from the church ladies.

A few months later, when Dorie moved back in with her mama and daddy, and her middle had grown larger than any other part of her body, I figured out why she needed a sack dress at her wedding. Dorie never did go back to that husband. Grandma said he was a no-count swamp rat who sent Dorie to work everyday, then drank up all her earnings.

"Mae," Grandma said one day, her eyes flashing, "don't you ever do something like Dorie done. Don't let men touch your bare body and get you all messed up."

I nodded, knowing I never wanted hands like Dorie's husband's and her daddy's to scratch me with their farm-roughened hide. It wasn't until some years later that my skin welcomed the touch of an oyster fisherman.

"What do you want from me, Mae?" Jack's urgency at pulling on his tee, then zipping his jeans filled me with guilt, a desperation, yet full expectation, that he'd walk away and I'd never deal with him again. "You play these games, send me packing, then grovel around in my bed..."

"My bed." I held onto the wooden bed poster like it would rise up and

float away from me. A Victorian thing, it was the first bed I'd ever owned and paid for with my own salary. I had a right to sleep with anyone I wanted in that bed.

"Your bed, my bed. It's not exactly our bed, is it?" *Jack grabbed my hairbrush and ran it through his thinning black hair. He would be beautiful bald, I told myself.*

"It's just that I need security, Jack, a knowledge that I'm not going to have to support someone. It's this fear I have."

"Your grandma's fear, you mean." *He turned and faced me. Jack, the handsomest man I'd ever seen, actually loved me, even wanted to marry me. He placed his hands on his thin hips, his jaw and biceps clenching and unclenching in his anger. Black eyes glared at me, the same ones that shined like ebony rock when he smiled.*

"I'm never going to be rich, Mae, not by oyster fishing. But I'm stable and will make the best husband you're ever going to get."

"I know, I know." *I let the tears fall. I felt as though my body were crushing into the wall, becoming a part of dead wood.*

"Give me time, Jack."

"Time for you to run to Grannie and let her tell you I'm not the marrying kind, that my daddy divorced twice, that I've had too many girlfriends?" *He threw his arms into the air, then turned around and slammed the door.*

I waited, leaning against the wall and hanging onto that bed poster for nearly twenty minutes. He had to come back. When he didn't, I fell onto the rumpled sheets, caressing his odor against my face.

He had come to me on my thirtieth birthday after not seeing me for weeks. Our currents ran fast and deep and we made love for nearly an hour. Three times, he stopped his rhythmic movements, took a deep breath, and held himself in the air. I glanced at him, fearing he had tired of me. He was looking at me, the frenzy and sweat of love-making around his forehead, and a questioning in his eyes. Three times, I shut my eyes against the truth and whispered, "Don't stop." But he did stop. Jack walked away from me and my bed poster, ran straight to Judy Lamath and married her. He's still married to her, and he's fat and really bald. I don't see him much, but when I do, he's got that wide grin. He didn't turn out to be a beautiful bald man.

"Lots of fish in that river," said Grandma when she heard Jack had married. "Go get you another one." She always looked at me sideways when she talked about me and men, like warning me not to sleep with them. She never talked about it, never had a four-letter word for it, but like the time I said pregnant in her presence, she wouldn't hear of anything like "making love." I never uttered it.

I found a few of those other fish. One, a Mr. Harold Campana, courted me like a knight. He courted Grandma, too, bringing her flowers and a bottle of bourbon in exchange for taking me down the river to a new shrimp restaurant. He danced. I guess I felt good in his arms, his expensive Italian suit stroking my face. Harold charmed me, even contented me, but I never desired anything beneath the suit. He persisted. I finally drank too many rums and decided to let him have me. He took me to a friend's beach house on the bay where the river meets the Gulf. He'd borrowed it for the evening. Outside, boats tied up at dock, and the twilight on the water sparkled inside my rummy head.

When Harold put on some old music, "Moon Over Miami," I think, I began to giggle.

"You do this all the time?" He passed me a glass of champagne.

"What?" I toasted him and sipped the bubbles.

"Giggle." He smiled at me, the darkness of his eyes and skin bringing out the stark white teeth. I stared at them for a minute and bet myself they weren't real. If he pulled them out at night, I planned on leaving—swimming back home if I had to.

I giggled again. "Only when I'm tickled about something," I said.

"Come over here." He pulled me by the hand and sat me on a plush sofa, propping me with pillows. "Have a shrimp." He had placed a platter of boiled shrimp and oysters on the half shell atop the round coffee table. Lift-

ing the peeled shrimp, he placed it in my mouth. As I chewed, he chewed something invisible, like mocking me. He took an oyster, tilted it into my mouth. I pushed myself into the pillows and giggled until my eyes blurred.

"What's all that light?" I could see spots of light around the room, like little space ships flying about my head.

"Candles. Do you like them?"

I nodded and smiled. He placed another oyster in my mouth.

"I've heard shellfish are aphrodisiacs," I said and imagined the slimy things slithering down my throat all the way to my genitals. I wanted to bust, to laugh and roll on the floor, but I made sexy talk instead.

"Come on," he said and took the champagne glass from me. The bedroom had become a fire hazard. Lit candles surrounded the bed, giving the place a funereal look. Harold kissed my neck. His lips, cold and wet, made me think he had slipped one of the iced oysters down my dress. When I jumped, he pulled, and I sat on the edge of the bed in my underwear. He crawled across the king-size on his knees and unhooked my bra. When I wouldn't move, he told me to "get out of those," meaning my panties.

"What about you?" I turned to undo his shirt.

Harold pushed my hand away. "Just a minute." He left the bed and went to a dark corner. I could hear the shirt, then the belt, and finally the zip of the pants. He didn't return right away. I imagined him slipping off his jockeys and socks. The rum and champagne combined in my head like gremlins. Between my legs, I felt none of the excited tingling urgency I'd had with Jack. Instead, I giggled and reached toward the bed table. When I heard the faint rustle of sheets as Harold approached, I switched on the light.

"Ah! Damn it, turn that off." He waved the air like he didn't know which part of his body to cover first. It didn't matter. It was already covered. He qualified for the missing link, gorilla man, with long straight hair tufts from his ankles to his neckline. The process of removing his shirt made it stand straight up from the skin on his back. In the dim light, I couldn't see any fleshy color at all. I was about to be embraced by an ape.

"Kong! You made it through the window!" It came out, along with rum, champagne, and oysters. I hurled it all on the floor. Sometime later, I borrowed a boat and motored to Grandma's alone. Grandma snored in her chair, drunk on bourbon but waiting up just in case.

I hadn't had a bit of alcohol, not even a bottle in the cooler, but I laughed out loud, echoing down the river, until I had tears in my eyes. I rested then, even slept, I think. Something changed in the river water. The current eased as though listening for an intruder. The only anhinga bird I had seen today took off like he'd been kicked into orbit. I sensed someone around me, maybe in the swamp, but there just the same. When I heard a rhythmic rowing I thought The Ageless Hippies might be coming my way instead of their planned route.

When the rowing stopped, I turned. Nothing behind me, nor in front. On each side the cypress trees reached into the water like monsters. Some were thick and grew in groves of water lilies and hyacinth flowers. A chill set over me, and I wanted to hurry back to the women on the river bank, to safety. I pulled into a shade of oak branches and waited. Nothing happened, not even a frog croaked. I looked up the bank where a long alligator sunned himself. He didn't move.

I focused across the river in the cypress trees that rose out of the water as though they had been baptized. A shadow, white and man-made, passed behind a tree. I could see a hand using the tree trunk as a balance. Whoever was there stood in the boat. I leaned forward to peer through the moss. River lights play tricks on you. What seems to be a swimming alligator could be a group of lily pads moving with the current. The white hand on the tree could be a giant fungus, and the end of the boat, debris that had coasted against the trees.

"You lost, lady?" The voice came from behind me.

I nearly fell into the water. I rocked the boat precariously as I scrambled to find the canister of pepper spray. When I had it in my hand, I turned around from one side to the other. The origin of the voice alluded me. When the gator slid off the bank into the river, I focused on the shore. In the trees, I saw the old bush hook fisherman. He grinned. The rifle in his hand could have blown me into fish bait. I had trapped myself inside the limb cover.

I ducked, willing to go overboard and swim with the gator. When I dared peep over the edge of the boat, I saw the man trotting into the trees, pushing back into the jungle from where he came. I jerked my head toward the image across the river just in time to see a boat disappear into a cove. The man didn't row, but pushed the boat with a long stick in one hand. Even from the back, I would have sworn it was Old Joe.

VIII

"Old Joe, you're just the nail in my four walls," Grandma fanned gnats away from Joe as he snored in his swing. "Place would fall down around me without you."

"Grandma, are you married to Joe?" I dared ask the question, the one my school friends whispered about because their parents whispered about it.

"Let me be, girl." Grandma sent me her pat answer along with the threatening gaze. "Thankful we got him." She'd look back at the silent man who wore overalls long after they were nearly impossible to buy.

"Got to order overalls for Joe," Grandma would say at Christmas as she made out the catalog order. "Don't want him running around the swamp bare-assed." She'd take a swig from the Mason jar then look down at me, "Oops! Don't hear me say those words, Mae. Just listen to the whooping cranes."

"Not any whooping right now," I'd chime in. Sometimes Grandma would laugh. Others, she would glare at me like I had encroached on her humor.

"I'm taking a nap. Don't gab at me now," Grandma would say and drift off to her room at the back of the wood frame. Sunday chicken and dumplings and her Mason jar guaranteed she wouldn't wake up before three.

"Get the radio on," Joe said, his eyes still closed and the swing still swaying. "Listen to Gene Aw-ter-ee." The waltz cadences emanating from

Gene Autry's guitar and vocal chords inspired Joe to smile, then to stand up and offer me his hands. I climbed up from the front step and put both my hands in his palms. He guided me into the living room, then placed my little girl arm on his right forearm and held onto my right hand. He swayed first, in time to the music, his eyes closed with that silly grin. I could smell the faint damp tobacco odor he had about his clothes. When the grin opened and became a snuff-stained smile, we moved. Little girl and big overall-clad Joe shuffled across the linoleum in waltz time. Joe's bare feet rustled as he slid his callouses over the floor in a four-square pattern, his strides growing bigger and bigger with each Autry refrain.

I followed, light-footed, and believed myself a fairy princess who danced in a castle with her prince. That prince, like Joe, would smile at me, protect me, and ask nothing more than I care to dance with him. When my prince's stride got too wide for me, he lifted me up and swung me around in perfect rhythm. My entire being thrilled at this, and I believed Joe could make me fly.

One time Joe turned on the radio and got the wrong station. The college station played mostly classical, and this time the Strauss waltzes sounded inside the wood and linoleum house. He stopped, then turned to me, and in one of his rare moments of verbal creativity, said, "Let's do the big city waltz today. Give Aw-ter-ee a rest." He raised himself full height, tilting his nose into the air. I did the same, took his arm and hand, and followed him around the room while the "Blue Danube" flowed across the air. Joe's feet lifted off the floor this time, no rustling sound, but no shoes, either. And this time, when he lifted me at the end of the music, he tilted me over. My head nearly touched the floor, while my back rested over one knee. When Strauss hit the finale, he pulled me up again with the grace of a ballet dancer, and stood me square on the floor. Our arms and hands were still in position for the next waltz.

Later in the evening when Grandma served us leftover chicken and a biscuit with honey, she said, "What happened to Autry? He helps me sleep. Didn't hear him today."

I looked at her in shock. For the first time I realized she knew all along we danced in the living room while she slept off a liquor haze.

"Got the big time today," said Joe. He turned his ill-shaven face in my direction, grinned to show crumbled biscuit, and winked. I wrapped my arms around myself to keep in the giggling warmth I felt. These two people and I had our Sunday afternoon secrets, and I knew they were safe.

"Does Little Miss Alligator do the waltz?" I said as I pressed a half biscuit into a pool of syrup.

"All the time," said Grandma. "When she's not sleeping, of course." She glanced at Joe with that knowing look in her eyes. He winked at her, too.

Poor Joe, I thought as I sat in the boat. One side all weak with the stroke. He'd never be able to lift me now, not even if I was still a little girl. Joe taught me more than boxing my feet to the waltz. Once, when I was nearly twelve, he took me to the river bank and showed me a canoe he'd bought off some fisherman in need of beer money.

"You ought to know how to handle yourself in the water, girl." He held the canoe as I got in, then said to watch him shove it off from the bank. "Ain't hard, but you got to push so it gets the momentum and goes straight without rocking side to side."

I practiced with Joe until I could shove off "just like an Indian chief," he said. Then came the rowing. My developing arms ached at night from the repetitious movement with the oars, rowing first with one oar, then with two, learning to turn, to keep a steady course. Then came turning the canoe over and getting back in while in deep water. Overcoming my fear of rocking the canoe until it tipped me out caused me the most anxiety. Turning it over in the water, balancing myself on the side and falling back in required the most dexterity. "Now, if you fall out, you can rescue yourself and the boat," said Joe. "But what you gonna do if you lose the oars when it tips over?" He answered by placing his big hand in the water, cupping the palm and slowly moving the canoe around with oar-like movements. "Hand paddle, but only as long as it takes you to get to shore."

I managed to go in circles for nearly an hour before I got the hang of using both hands to guide the canoe to the bank. Not two years later, I found myself in a predicament. Taking an inner tube to the swimming area on the river, where the water ran clear and the white sand sloped rather than dropped to deep waters, I'd hope to meet some of Miz Stasia's daughters. A few boys were there, swinging from vines and causing a great racket in the water. I pushed the tube into the river and climbed on, my butt dipping into the water, my legs and shoulders resting on the rim. Looking upward, the bright sun rays shot through cypress and oak branches, giving the river a strobe light effect. I closed my eyes against the glare.

When I awoke, I was mid-river, far from the boys on the vines. I could have swum, I suppose, using the tube as a float, but my first instinct was to reach over with my hands and guide the inner tube to shore. Within a few minutes, I had beat the strong current and rubbed against a muddy bank. Struggling out of the tube, I grabbed hold of the rim, and dragged it to the swamp. That proved the most difficult—walking through pure forest to find the road back to Grandma's.

Nothing frightened me then. Nothing but Grandma. When I reached the house, I sneaked up to the hose and rinsed the mud off me and the tube, then went in the back door to change. No one ever knew.

I shoved out of the grove to the center of the river. I vowed to keep a vigil on the shore line for any signs of a Gruman and his rifle. I even took to zig-zagging the boat when the paranoia of being shot with the aid of a scope got to me. In a few more miles, I'd be at Miz Stasia's and again wrapped in safety. I used the motor, but moved slowly. It was Saturday, a day for half the city people to drag out their garage boats and scoot down the river just to say they did it.

I never could tell what they actually did on the river. Too full of trees and underwater hazards to ski, and the locals took up all the fishing. Alligators gave up sunning on a busy day like this. Soon as they got a comfortable spot, the noisy motor came alongside them, stopping suddenly. The wake splashed onto their tails. Lifting himself on four stubby legs, the gator turned around, then slid face first into the cool water. If you could see him at all, he'd skim along the surface until he got to a patch of leaf debris that covered the river surface, then pop his eyes and nostrils up just above the water line to survey the world.

Miz Stasia—short for Anastasia—arrived in the swamps from Greece when she was three years old. Her parents, old-world Greeks, found a place to build a boathouse and took to fishing in the Gulf. They sold mullet, grouper, oysters, and shrimp wholesale to the fish markets in Tallahassee until Stasia's eldest son got smart enough to open his own market. The family grew to seven children, but only Stasia stayed on in the boathouse.

Her parents called over a young Greek sailor they knew from the old country and married her off, figuring they'd have plenty of grandchildren. And they did. George and Anastasia Skourous produced ten healthy offspring who spoke Greek and Southern, and mixed baklava with pecan pie. When George died in a boating accident around their fifteenth anniversary, Stasia sat back in her rocker on the boathouse and said, "I'm going to enhance this place."

She left the over-the-water section and added a two-story behind it. Beyond that, she removed trees to form a large circular clearing where her kids could do the bop and the elders could circle dance to the old Greek tunes.

Stasia spoke Southern just like my grandma. The two of them became fast friends, two lone women who lived in the river swamp. Grandma's body grew taut and wiry like a thick vine that hung from an ancient oak. Stasia widened at the bottom. Her top held up tremendous breasts that she pushed further up with what she called a "straight-jacket bra." An earth mother, her dark eyes and hair set off dewy olive skin. Shoes irritated her. Her wide-spaced toes on flat feet, forever bare, walked across the forest floor, cold linoleum, wooden decking, and finally into black mud at the river's edge.

Even if you didn't know her, from the shape of her body you'd surmise Stasia had a pile of kids. Now she has a pile of grandkids, even one or two great-grandkids. On Sundays, they swarm over her boathouse and addition, dart off the swamp roads like termites to logs and herd into the circular clearing where the women set up long tables of potato salad, collard greens, pastitsio, dholmas, feta cheese, and Greek olives. Fish comes fried in corn meal or soaked in lemon sauce. And oysters swim down throats, slimy from the shell, often chased by anisette. Music plays from noon to deep into the night. Twangy country-western guitars back up lonesome trail singers until the blasting electric instruments of hard rock take over. Finally, someone picks up the bouzouki and strums out "Zorba's Dance." Then the line dances begin, and western-born males become Greek again, twisting and turning as they hold the handkerchief between them. Kneeling, slapping the leg, and swaying sexually to the sounds, they recapture the land of Homer in all its Dionysian splendor.

Greek wine flows down throats along with bourbon and Coke. Often, one of Miz Stasia's descendants ends up in the river long enough to sober up. To be invited to one of these Sunday outings required being on nearly sisterly terms with Miz Stasia. Not even her granddaughters could bring their dates before declaring their engagement. "Too many mouths to feed already," she'd say and brush away the devastated teen.

Grandma had a standing invitation, but she almost never came. "Your grandma don't like many people around her at one time," she once told me. "And that Old Joe, he never wants to come."

But I wanted to come. I steered the boat through a side branch of the river, a narrow alley of deep water and low-hanging magnolia trees. The lane widened into a Southern painting. The old boat house with its flat roof and wooden deck still floated in the cove. Behind, a two-story, green-shuttered, white mansion rose into the oak trees. A string of parked cars and trucks lined the sparse woods next to the water. As I tied up, I watched dark-haired preteens chase about between forest pines, tossing cones at each other. In the distance, a boom box blasted high-pitched rock guitars. I waited, allowing the sounds and scents to give up their ghosts.

"Take care of little Georgie," said Stasia as she sent him off to play in the creek with his two older sisters. "Don't let him get too close that he falls in."

They skipped off through the woods with empty tin cans to collect tadpoles, kneeling next to the water on dark sand that must have been near black on the creek bottom. Out there, in the dark creek, the older kids would swing off tree branches and land in the darkness only to surface downstream and climb upon a floating log. There were no kids there that day, only two girls under twelve and one little boy with large black eyes and the namesake of his Greek father.

"I got my jars filled," said one sister. "Mama ain't much going to like live frogs developing inside the house." They laughed and imitated fat Stasia jumping about, yelling that dried frogs didn't belong in the baklava. Their

silliness grew self-centered, and they forgot about Georgie on the bank. Forgot, until he cried out in pain.

The doctor said it was a water moccasin bite and too late to save the arm. It had swollen to the size of a baseball bat and turned black. The eldest boy in the Skourous family would live his life without a left arm below the elbow.

I heard this story about Georgie off and on over the years, first from his sisters, then from Grandma. It never played like a tragedy. Losing an arm gave Georgie an out from harvesting the sea. He went to college, instead, got a degree in business, then opened the first seafood store.

"Made the family rich," said Stasia. "Good comes out of just about everything."

And Georgie was good. Long before he did his growing into adulthood, he became the teller of swamp tales, the kind where ghosts hang on moss strands. All his sisters and I loved to gather round him in the clearing behind the big house, around a bonfire, on a foggy night and listen to what was out there. Georgie often included his missing arm in the tales.

"See the ghosts creeping about," he'd whisper and point a finger to the spaces between trees where fog had accumulated into ectoplasm. "Sometimes they're good and just like to tease. But, when you hear a screech owl and a Florida panther on the same night, look out! That's what happened the night before I lost my arm. Something evil rose out of the river and hid in with the fog ghosts. It unwound itself from a big cypress knee clump and crept slowly up on the bank like a gator with cat eyes. Found a spot in the deep grass just there at the top of the creek bank. Ate himself a few toad frogs." Georgie would use his remaining hand to dart out like a striking snake and bite at the girls.

We screamed in terror and huddled against each other. "That something turned itself into a fat, black moccasin with five inch fangs, just waiting for a bare foot to come skipping down to the creek." Since we wore no shoes, we scrunched up our toes and hid them underneath our dresses. "Long about noon, demon snake got too hot. He slithered to the creek and scooped up some tadpoles on his black forked tongue. Then he rolled round in the water, kicking up the black sand and blinding all the minnows. By that time, he wasn't too interested in eating something tiny. He raised that ugly head and looked around the surface like a submarine scope. Got his eye focused on this little boy up on the bank. Looked like juicy, tender meat to him. So," Georgie drew the word out, his eyes widening in fear. "he slithered onto shore, just a few feet away from some little girls who played in the shallows. Quietly," Georgie lowered his voice; we leaned forward, "he swayed his body up the hill, moving between tufts of grass. Then he got about three feet from the boy, his low beady eyes seeing a bare knee move in the grass. He wanted that knee; he undulated toward it." None of us knew the word undulated, but Georgie would make snaky movements with his body and dart his tongue about. "Just inches in front of the knee, the boy decided to get up. He put down his hand to shove himself off the ground and landed hand-to-nose with demon snake. Well, in seconds that snake decided hand would be more tender than knee. He struck, those five inch fangs digging into the back of the little boy's hand."

We grabbed our own wrists and held on for dear life. "Snapped that kid's hand right off! You know what he did next? He liked the taste. He opened wide and gulped down the whole kid. Lay there with a bulge in his body for half a day. Nobody ever saw that kid again." We stared, silent, wondering what it would be like to find oneself in the darkness of a snake's belly. "Now, when the fog ghosts come dancing around your window, better get under the covers, head and all. That little boy is still out there, and some say you can hear him crying for his mama. You got to listen hard in the fog, when the animals go quiet. Listen!" He stopped talking, and not a one of us moved.

For some reason, the crickets and frogs made no noise either, and the swamp mists thickened around us. Georgie held up his stub and began to rub it, making little breathing sounds like it pained him. We focused on it, afraid to look at the gathering fog or into the night behind us. Georgie raised his head with a jerk and stared off into the woods, his eyes bulging, his mouth slightly ajar. No one moved.

"Whaaaaaaaa!" Georgie screamed in a voice like no animal we'd ever heard. We screeched. Leaping over each other and darting through the fog to the house, we took refuge around Stasia's heavy body like chicks nudging under a mother hen's feathers. We slept with the sheet over our heads. When dawn came, the odor of ham slabs and biscuits drew us downstairs. The night demons had left us with our arms intact.

"Miz Stasia about?" I asked a wide-eyed boy of about six, looking much like little Georgie with both arms.

He had come to the dock to watch me steady the boat. He pointed to the yard behind the big house. "She's putting 'keercomb on Sally," he said, referring to the red antiseptic used for cuts and bites in the South.

Holding the foil-wrapped pound cake in my hands, I climbed out of the boat. Glancing back, I wondered if Grandma would be safe with this many children. "What's your name?" I asked the boy.

He stood on the landing with his hands clasped behind his back. "Teddy."

"Well, Teddy, I'm appointing you official guard of the royal boat there." I stood straight as a soldier and pointed. "You are to let no one go aboard, no one at all. Got that?"

Teddy nodded, his eyes wide and unblinking. I was pretty sure he wouldn't let anyone on the boat, but something told me he might try to get there himself. Miz Stasia's place, an ant bed of activity on a Sunday afternoon, disturbed the calm of the swamp. No snakes or alligators or deer would bless these banks with their presence for several hours. From the darting, screaming small ones near the banks to the adolescents who tossed balls or dabbled in cheap make-up kits through the new parents who nursed babies and rested in folding plastic-plaid chairs, I made my way to the kitchen and Stasia. She stood near the door that opened into an expansive living room. Around her, daughters and their daughters and her sons' wives banged pots of baked beans, grated cole slaw, layered pasta over spiced meat and broke goat cheese into salads.

Stasia, in a black dress that hung low at the neck and tightened around her hips, held a soiled apron in one arm. Her feet, wide-toed and dirty, were bare. "Mae!" she cried when she saw me and came forward with outstretched arms that reminded me of the days when she did the circle dances with the men. In a locking embrace, she greeted me. She smelled of cornmeal and olive oil.

My body pressed against hers, she felt surprisingly soft and lumpy. I pushed back. "Oh! You noticed," she cried. "I threw away all my straight-jacket bras. At seventy-six, I don't wear one at all. Now how about that!"

I laughed with her, silently envying her self-security, the freedom she had earned. I handed her Aunt Becky's pound cake.

"Oh, that Becky child." She still saw Aunt Becky as a little girl who came to play with Stasia's oldest sister. "She always did the best baking." She went to a refrigerator that had seen its heyday in the early fifties and placed the wrapped cake on top. "My stuff only," she said and took me by the hand out the back door. "You must be starving. The tables are still full and will get fuller when those women stop messing about and get the pans out here. Help yourself."

Joined-together wooden tables, covered with white plastic cloths, filled the length of one end of the clearing. A few feet away, men squatted with paper plates; women leaned against pine trunks or unfolded napkins and covered the brown straw to make a ground seat. Younger people plopped right on the straw, crossing their legs. Between bites, they conversed, some in Greek, most in the familiar Southern drawl of Northern Florida.

Pulling a paper plate from a tall clear plastic bag, I paraded down one side of the table alignment. Long Pyrex dishes held the fragrant Greek delicacies laced with eggplant, grape leaves, spiced meat, and pasta custards. Thick Greek bread lay in a pile beside thin strips of roasted meat, shredded lettuce, and yogurt sauce. A red-haired woman who spoke no English plopped down a plate of round fried chickpea fritters—falafel, she said. We rolled these up in the bread with the sauce for a Greek gyro, or moved on down the table where we pulled off chunks of roast pork and pushed them into the bread, washing it down with iced tea. Tall plates of fried chicken went faster than anything else, until the coconut custard pie and baklava hit the dessert table. I started light, with a Greek salad of lettuce, olives, feta, and anchovies, and a spoonful of cheese grits.

"You come up here and eat beside me," said Stasia. She waved me to two rocking chairs at one end of the porch, away from the kitchen door and flow of cooks and children.

I sat in the rocker, letting it move me gently back and forth before I stopped to eat. Closing my eyes, I remembered this place when Grandma would bring me over and sit me here while she spoke to Stasia inside the kitchen. Stasia would hand me a piece of honey-tasting candy and tell me to watch for snakes in the yard. Usually, one of her grandkids came by and sat in the other chair and stared at me until I felt guilty and handed her a piece of the candy. She rarely ate it.

"Your grandma," Stasia said as she heaved herself into the rocker. With a bare foot, she dragged a wicker stool from under the chair and placed both feet on top. Her legs seemed the same size from the knees to the toes. "I was sorry to hear of her passing. You got the flowers we sent?"

I nodded and took a spoon of grits into my mouth.

"She were the kindest—no, I won't say that. It's not true." She laughed to herself. "Guess your grandma was the most unusual person I knowed. Gave my life excitement." She looked at me suddenly.

I nodded my head in the direction of a circle of toddlers fighting over a cat who wanted nothing but to run into the forest. We both burst into laughter.

"Oh, Stasia, it's good to be here," I said and leaned back, suddenly disinterested in eating.

"Look at me, Mae." Stasia leaned over, her breasts flopping to either side of her stomach. The black dress was low enough to reveal deep cleavage. In spite of her years, her dewy skin had only traces of stretch marks and no dark age spots. "What's wrong?"

"Can I bunk here tonight?" I felt a lump in my throat; my eyes watered.

"Beds are all taken, but you can put a bag on the deck like you used to." Stasia said the right words. In my teens, I preferred to stay here or with Grandma when Aunt Becky visited relatives in Alabama. At first, Stasia tucked me in with a granddaughter, but I didn't like that. The girl kicked at night. In the summers, I took to bringing a sleeping bag and bedding down on the wooden floors of her screened deck.

"That will be perfect, Stasia." My lumpy throat allowed only a whisper.

Stasia unwrinkled her brow, moved her feet off the stool, and patted my hand. "You eat now. When most of this crew has left, you come and talk to me."

Stasia, the embracer, hearer of the deepest confessions, had been my grandmother's best friend, as far as I knew. I often wondered how this could be. Surely Grandma, who never shared an intimacy with me in her life, would find this woman of Greek passions an intrusion.

I filled myself with pastitsio and fried chicken wings, pita and pork roast, then joined a line dance. One of the recent arrivals from Greece had had enough of loud rock and switched off the boom box. The toddlers lay on blankets spread on the porch and slept, while the teens filled themselves with soda and dreamed of exercising their hormones. The Greek man pulled out his bouzouki, a long banjo-looking instrument, and began to play. His cousin retrieved a drum from his shabby truck and sat on the porch steps. The loud, exotic chords sounded through the swamp, bringing forth a longing for white Mediterranean houses and warm ocean breezes.

An elderly man pulled a handkerchief from his pocket and held it aloft. Another grabbed hold, then men and women took hands and held up their right knees in unison. We stepped, twisted at the waist, bent out knees, then repeated it over and over again as the music intensified. The man at the front of the line moved into the circle and slapped his foot, bent, then squatted, then rose again in a passion passed down from gods long forgotten in the Bible belt of North Florida.

I let the music take me, drifting in rhythm with the others. My feet, unaccustomed to the steps, followed as if they had their own guidance systems. For a moment, Gruman and that boy in the ruined shed disappeared.

IX

"You come round to the boat deck," said Stasia as she waved to the last relative who would spend the night in one of the bedrooms in the big house. "That's my private place now. I got a right to it after all these kids and their kids. Won't nobody disturb us. Get yourself a tea and meet me there."

Night frogs croaked their feeding songs as they zapped mosquitoes with sticky tongues and dodged Little Miss Alligator's jaws. Trees and moss hung thick over the water, blocking out the moonlight except for patches where the river reflected shiny darkness. If you sat perfectly still, you might hear the deep currents racing through limestone caves, a sort of river whistle, low and filled with life.

There had been a time after Jack when I wanted to join those whistles, to let my body travel with the current under the river—lifeless yet offering life. I had come to realize that I wanted his maleness, needed it, in the form of heavy arms, scent and sex, but I didn't want him. When I thought of long days in a linoleum-floored house, waiting for him to return from an oyster boat, then feeding him, comforting him, watching him drop off in front of a television only to wake up early and be off on the boat again, I saw a narrow, endless tunnel. I turned it all off, made sure he'd go away and put someone else in that scenario. The string of men to follow never matched him, and I knew then I'd never marry. "You still working for the state?" Stasia sat in a wooden rocker and propped her feet on an empty orange crate. She knew where I worked. She just offered an opening for deep talk.

"If you call it work," I said. "There's something of sameness about it. It's more like motion, like a pendulum. Given the right balance, it'll keep swinging, mindlessly, forever."

"Oh, honey, I hear a bitterness." Stasia's eyes would have widened, black on a pudgy face surrounded by her white hair, if I could have seen them in the dark.

"I get that way when someone dies, I guess. Right now that job seems like a safety clause in my life."

Stasia shifted her weight in the rocker. She pulled up her dress to expose her knees to the humid night air. "You know, getting old hasn't been bad except for these legs and feet of mine." I heard her take a tin from under the chair, open it, and spread the waxy substance across her knees. It was some concoction sent from Greece. "I'm sorry I didn't make it to your grandma's funeral," she said. "It's just too hard to put on shoes and get all spruced up."

"No one expected you to be there, Stasia. You know that."

"Still, she was my friend from way back when we were little girls."

"Did you know my grandfather, Stasia?" Crickets turned up their grinding, piercing the darkness like screeching violins.

Stasia listened to them a long time before she spoke. "No, I never met him. Your grandma went away about the time I got married off to a Greek. When I saw her again, she had two small boys and lived in that river house. Said her husband died of a flu fever. I had more than two kids by then and stayed busy. I never really talked to her about it. Then, Joe started coming round here with her. I never pried. Why you want to know?"

"Could I be Joe's granddaughter?" Stasia rubbed her other leg hard enough for her hand to rasp against the skin. I could hear her breathing hard as though she had walked up stairs. "Some have said that." The rubbing continued.

"Do you believe it?"

"No."

"Stasia, I'm old enough now—forty-five—tell me the truth."

"I don't think you're any relation to Joe. If those two boys, your papa and Uncle Nast, had been Joe's, he would have married your grandma. He's a good man, that Joe, even if he's a simple creature of the swamp. He never let her down."

"Did you know someone named Skipper, an old man about Joe's age, I think?"

Stasia chuckled and leaned back, the salve still on her fingers. "Don't you remember old Skipper Lou? You and Anya, must have been the first full naked male body either of you saw."

Anya, Stasia's third daughter, was my physical opposite. Me, strawberry-red hair and freckles; her, black hair and olive skin. Once, Grandma and Stasia decided to visit Hannah Haga way back in the swamp for some herbs to cure impetigo sores. Stasia's kids were having a time with it, and the city doctors weren't doing much good.

Hannah Haga, a black woman of uncertain age, lived in a shack in the woods.

She was a holdover from slave days when those slave women who got too old to be useful were turned out to a cabin in the woods. Out of necessity, they took up using nature for food and medicine. Combining that with their heri-

tage from slavery and Africa, they became witches or voodoo women. Today, they would be herbalists.

I saw Hannah Haga only once in my life. Grandma took me with her to the wood store up near the fork on Saturday afternoon. We rowed nearly all the way there. Grandma, tired and sweaty, sat in the back and chatted with the owner. I roamed the wood floors, dragging my hands across the bolts of flannel and sifting shiny nails between my fingers. When the bell over the door rang, the owner came out from a curtained doorway and said niceties to the customer. I backed between the bins of soap and peanuts and raw rice, and watched. No one knew I was there until the day I backed into a dark corner. A chair rocked there and I thought it was a ghost until I saw the whites of eyes glance up at me. I moved closer where I found an ancient woman who smelled of turpentine. Dressed in various brown colors, her head covered in a kerchief, she seemed part of a tree. I had visions of lightning striking a giant pine, splitting it open and popping out a black human, black enough to blend in with the night.

Hannah sat in a rocker, but she didn't sway. On the floor beside her, she lifted pine needles from a paper sack. With her ebony fingers that looked like burnt wood from a campfire, she wove the straw back and forth, around and around, then bound them together with a needle and thick thread. I stood in front of her, staring, mesmerized by the dark fingers and their rhythmic movement that formed a pine-straw basket.

After some minutes, she stopped to glance up at me. She grinned, exposing one tooth on the bottom of her mouth. Then she sucked on the tooth, reached into the bag, and continued her hand weaving. When the basket had partial sides, Hannah Haga eyed me again. "That your grannie back there?" Her voice whispered like somebody sawing in the distance.

I nodded. She leaned forward and grabbed my arm with the burnt black fingers. "You tell her to buy a basket, okay?" With her other hand, she reached behind the chair and picked up a pine-straw bowl the size of a coffee cup, its brown needles tightly woven and held together with green thread.

I took the basket then looked back at Hannah. She had resumed her weaving like I had never been there at all. Later, I held the basket up to Grandma. She nodded like she knew it all, dropped some coins in Hannah's lap and left the store.

The four of us—Grandma, Stasia, Anya, and I—boated far up the river, almost to the fork, then back into a watery lane to a natural docking place. From the boat, we could see the outline of a gray-wood shack. The oily odor coming from the shack drifted on foggy smoke through the trees. "You girls wait in the boat now," said Grandma. She and Stasia climbed the bank with a sack of jars.

Anya and I looked at each other in the quiet, smoke and smell surrounding us. "Is she a witch?"

"Don't know. Grandma says she's wise."

"My brother says she's lived just about forever."

I shrugged, not having any more hearsays to add. "Wonder who lives up there." I pointed to a cleared path on the other side of the water lane. The shore there was shallow and clear enough to swim in. Anya leaned over to look through the trees, then let her fingers drift in the water by the boat. She lifted a lily pad but it wouldn't pull loose, and she let it flop back into the water.

"I wish we could go swimming over there," she said. Before I could answer, we heard whistling. Then a man appeared on the lane. He wore a denim shirt over nothing, his bare white legs poking long and skinny to the ground. Anya and I held our giggles and ducked into the bottom of the boat. The man tossed a white cloth onto the tree branches, then threw a bar of floating soap into the water. Pulling off his shirt, he stood there in whiteness.

To this day, the part that struck me the oddest was the suntan marks on his arms and neck, and the rest of his body a ghostly pale. The man stretched, took deep breaths, grasped a hand cloth and jumped into the water. He gave a little whoop then ducked his whole head underneath, grabbing the cake of soap as he went down. When he came up, he moved closer to shore where he soaped himself all over. When he reached his crotch, he tossed his maleness about like a ping-pong paddle ball.

"What is that?" Anya whispered. I shook my head, unable to find words for something I knew I shouldn't see.

The man splashed back into the water, rolling like a gator to wash himself free of suds. Then he lathered his hair and went under twice to rinse. When he had done with his cleansing, he lay back and floated, his full front exposed to the sky—and to Anya and me. When he heard Stasia and Grandma talking on the way back to the boat, he scrambled to shore and pulled on the denim shirt. It stuck to his wet skin, prominently revealing his scrotum.

"Good day, ladies," he called, drying his hair with the white cloth. The rest turned into squeals of fright and giggles and curses toward a nasty old man. Later in the night, I lay in bed listening to Stasia and Grandma sipping from the jars and laughing until they nearly cried.

"Skipper Lou must be an antique by now," said Stasia as she laughed again. "He was always old, or maybe we just thought he was since he lived like a hermit."

"Did you know the Gruman family?"

"Now don't tell me you think one of them could be your grandpa." Stasia eased back in her chair. I could see her profile, rounded and homey, in the pale light.

"One of them came to the funeral."

Stasia rocked, her head tilted back and silent. I thought she may have fallen asleep. "That would have been Toller. Man about fifty, snide-looking."

"Yes. Why would he want to bid Grandma farewell?"

Stasia laughed. "Your forty-five years ain't taught you much, has it? He wasn't there to say bye." She chuckled gently then faded into silence.

"Stasia?"

"He probably went there to make sure she was dead."

The mugginess suddenly turned to cold. I couldn't rock any longer. Before I could say anything, a flashlight and voices appeared on the side of the porch.

"Stasia," said one of her sons-in-law, "we can't find Teddy. He didn't come when we called and he's not in bed with the others." I leaped from the rocker to the steps, nearly making a hole in the screen door, and darted toward the landing. My boat, still tied, rocked gently in the natural wake of the current. "Give me a light."

I shined the beam downward, silently praying that I wouldn't find a little Greek-eyed boy floating face down. I ran the light up the boat. There, at the end where Grandma sat, lay Teddy, asleep, curled around the brass urn. I relaxed, my shoulders sagging in relief. "He took me literally when I said watch the boat."

I pulled the urn from his arms, lifted my sleeping bag away, and made way for Teddy's parents. We followed Teddy's dad as he carried the little sentinel upstairs to a large room. Stasia had spread a wide spanse of blanket-covered foam on the bare floor, then tossed pillows about. Six children no bigger than Teddy claimed a spot and would sleep—like baby gators—under the protection of their elders.

"Some say your grandma had something to do with Toller's daddy's disappearance." We sat silently in the rocking chairs again, watching the moon dance on the river. "Others say she had everything to do with it."

As I sat the urn and bag at my feet on the porch, something jumped inside my head. A far-off, long ago sound of big people moving around me, of Grandma leaving for a trip and others rushing to help her.

I have always heard that small children sense when things are wrong, when a crisis is about, but I didn't know those senses returned. "Your grandma hated those Gruman men like a cat a dog," said Stasia. "She steered clear of them and took her gun every time she went out on the river." She turned her head to me. In the shadows, it appeared a round ball, a live snow creature. "All that happened after Old Man Gruman disappeared."

"He just vanished?"

Stasia nodded. "Sort of. He went out one night, full of whiskey, to gig frogs, he said. Those Gruman's still live off the swamp when they aren't hauling in fast food. Anyhow, not the man nor his gig nor his bag nor his clothes—nothing found."

"Why do they think Grandma had something to do with it?"

Stasia pushed back in the rocker like she was stretching her spine. "That night—when Gruman disappeared—Joe came through here. He wanted to borrow a boat. Said he'd banged his on a rock and got a leak. Now, Joe never is in a hurry. I'd think he'd just put his boat on shore and repair it the next day. But, no, he said he needed to put out bush hooks that night—after dark, mind you. I showed him a boat down there on the dock. He brought it back the next day."

"Why is that odd?"

"Well, first of all, he was mighty dirty, full of mud and leaves all up in his overalls, when he came to borrow the boat. Said he'd had to wade water to get the boat to shore."

"That's probably true."

"Then one of my boys asked him if he'd show him how to hang bush hooks. Now, Joe looked tired, but I guess he felt obligated. He said all right and took the boy out." Stasia stopped

River Whispers

talking to rock gently. Then she halted. "My boy said Joe didn't have any bush hooks out there, that he hadn't done any for a few days."

"You think he needed the boat for something else?"

"Well, your grandma sent me a note through the mail about a week later. Said she'd had to visit her cousin in Pensacola. Said Joe had run her down to the Bay Bridge where a friend drove her to the bus station."

"I didn't know there was a cousin in Pensacola."

"Wasn't, far as I know."

"Have you asked Joe?"

"Nope. He—or your grandma—would have told me if they wanted me to know."

"And this is somehow connected to the Gruman disappearance?"

"About the time Joe was out on the river with my boy, a Gruman came round here. Stood right there next to this porch with a rifle in one arm. Asked if I'd seen the old man, that he'd gone off gigging and might have had trouble. First thought most people had was that he fell in dead drunk and the gators had a liquor-laced cocktail. Then the other tales started."

"What tales?"

"Some say one of the Gruman women, one who married into the family, got raped by the old man. Some say that woman was your grandma's cousin, that she caught them and made alligator meat of Toller Gruman. Some say Old Joe helped her dispose of the body."

"Hogwash! My grandma? She was a small woman, strong, but not big enough to..." I couldn't finish it. I knew Grandma could do in anybody she wanted to. Her mind worked that way, took over and compensated for a lack of physical strength. "I never heard that about my grandmother."

"No, you wouldn't. Nobody talked about it around her or Old Joe, not ever. Plenty of talk in the woods, though. And in the old language." Stasia meant Greek. With her vast relatives, many who lived and worked on the bay, she would hear things and talk about them without whispering. "And the Grumans kept saying she had something to do with the whole thing."

"Why didn't this Gruman wife say something?"

"Woman packed up and left. Her husband took up with somebody else, and the sheriff found no trace of the old man. Back then, law people didn't do much of a job about somebody like Old Man Gruman. Most figured he weren't worth finding anyway." Stasia stretched her spine again and sighed. "But that family never stopped talking. They stopped looking for their daddy years ago and began grumbling about Miz Pope. Couldn't nobody prove it; it just fizzled. But, I imagine that's why the son come round to the funeral. One last poke, one last accusation."

I rested my eyes from glimpses of the river. I rocked along with Stasia, the runners sounding like a train across ties in the distance. My head swam, then focused on the old story.

"Little Miss Alligator got a boat oar and whacked that old bull across the head…"

And the old bull turned over and couldn't move. Little Miss Alligator pushed him off into the river where he drowned and was eaten by his fellow gators.

I opened my eyes wide. "Stasia," I whispered, "I saw something on my way here, something in the old fish camp up the river."

"Something Gruman, I suppose."

She didn't stop rocking.

"That man, the one at the funeral, he had this young boy. The boy looked sort of retarded. He pulled him into a shed in the rain and…"

"And rolled him over a log as we used to say?"

"How did you know?"

"The Gruman family is a bunch of hogs. Plenty of people told me about running across all kinds of nasty little incidents in these woods. We have to make sure we keep our people away from them, though they don't like to bother us—too many Greeks around to take revenge, I guess."

"But the boy," I had visions of the tortured face, silent in the pounding rain.

"More than likely one of their own. They don't much care, you know." She stretched her chubby arm and patted mine. "Don't fuss, Mae. It's them, not you. You could report it, but the sheriff ain't going to do anything. Can't without proof and won't none of them confess, not even the boy."

"It's a vision I won't get out of my head for a long time."

Stasia made a noise of agreement, then leaned back and began talking about Old Joe. "Your grandma knew him as a boy, a swamp boy, she says. He never made his living off the river like your grandma's people. Just farmed a little back inside the swamp—little tobacco, some vegetables, chickens, a cow or two. Never made much money, just enough to keep that little house in repair and eat. But he knows this swamp, Mae. Every inch, and he knows the Gruman family. Can tell you everyone of their names. Shoot! I don't even know how many are back there, but Joe does. He loved your grandma. She says he got all choked up and wouldn't come around anybody when she married. But soon as she come back, he's right there on her porch steps. Helped her raise your daddy and Nast. Most time when I went over there, Joe was there, too. If I had three-four kids with me, he'd take off for his house. Your grandma got a little testy with a bunch of kids about, too." Stasia chuckled. "Your grandma made a real woman, Mae. Sorry I didn't put on some shoes and make it to the funeral."

I leaned over and touched the urn. It shined in one spot where moonlight touched it. "She knows, Miz Stasia."

When Stasia finally raised herself and went through the screen door to the bedroom where she had conceived ten children, I pushed the rockers back and lay out my sleeping bag. With the moon higher in the sky, I could see river shadows better now. The mugginess rose off the water, a ghostly mist. Grandma sat near the steps, her urn glowing in the light. Night birds called occasionally, and crickets competed with frogs for concert time.

Along the screen, mosquitoes darted about, trying to find an opening large enough to let them in for their blood supply. I pulled off everything for the first time in two days. The humid breeze surrounded my body, making my skin jump with an itch every few minutes. I could feel sweat under my hair. I lifted it high off my neck. My feet, burning from wearing shoes, longed for a dip in the cool water. I slipped out the screen door and headed for the landing. The water at the end of the make-shift dock must have come from a spring somewhere nearby. It ran fast and clear.

I slipped in and drew my breath from the cold that slipped up my belly. I dipped underneath. Pure water engulfed my head, baptizing my spirit. I swam underneath, holding my breath for as long as I could. When I burst to the surface, I tread water then lay back and floated. Above me, oak limbs and their shadows swam around me. A cloud moved into my vision and blocked out the moonlight, casting the river like a watery grave. The animal noises stopped to let the cloud pass and began again when the moon came back.

The water felt comfortable now, no longer icy, and welcomed me as though I belonged. Then the cloud came again. Only this time, a light danced in the woods. It darted from tree to tree, making a line to a point somewhere near the boat house. I swam to the landing and held on to the post while I watched the light stop near Stasia's window. It circled round and came to rest on my boat. I ducked behind the post until the light moved off into the swamp. Later, I lay nude on my sleeping bag, my wet hair stretched out behind me. In the distance, I heard a baby gator wail and his mother roar in response. "Little Miss Alligator, your baby's in trouble," I whispered.

X

At five I woke to find Teddy standing over me. He stared at my naked body like he was seeing a new species of animal. I grabbed the sleeping bag and wound it around my front. "You're up early," I said.

He nodded. "Is your boat all right?" He pointed to the landing.

"Perfect," I said. "You did a great job, Teddy. You'll make a wonderful guard when you grow up."

"Sheriff," he grinned. "I'm going to be the sheriff."

"And I'll be in safe hands, for sure."

Teddy waved good-bye and ran inside the house. I heard his little feet echo across the linoleum until a door slammed somewhere.

Voices called "bye!" and "see you next Sunday." Stasia's family vacated the swamp early on Monday morning, heading for schools, jobs, and American routine. I lay on my left side on half the sleeping bag, wrapping the other half across my front. The air had only slightly cooled since last night, and the fog hovered, still, like risen river spirits gathering to greet Grandma. I couldn't see through the mist after about twenty feet. How could anyone see me?

From my position on the floor, I eyed Grandma's urn from the base to the slim stem attached to a large rounded bowl where the last of her ashes waited to be strewn about St. Margaret's River. The frogs and crickets quieted now, resting for the next round of solos. The baby gator had quit its wail hours ago. Either it flopped safely into the water or a giant white crane fed it to her chicks for breakfast.

I stayed like this, my face touching the old boards until they burned streaks on my skin. I felt the swamp around me, easing my spirit and making me know why Grandma belonged here. I drifted off to sleep and didn't wake again until a strong ray of sun flashed on my closed lids.

"You sleep okay out here?" Stasia sat in the rocker, balancing a cup of strong Greek coffee on the arm rest.

Sitting up, I felt the strain in one shoulder, the ache in the hip next to the floor. "Slept fine. God! I'm getting old." I stood, the bag draped around me, and listened to joints crack as though falling into place. "How long have you been sitting there?"

She didn't answer. "You're gonna want breakfast. And put on some clothes. Got a son or two who might drop by and put some fish in the freezer." Stasia left the porch and headed for the big kitchen in the add-on house.

I bent and felt pangs of soreness in my back.

"Good strong coffee will get those creaks out." Stasia poured from an old-world copper pot, bent and blackened from years of service. Then she dished out a large bowl of grits. I let the soft buttery mixture slide down my throat while she fried bacon and warmed biscuits. The small piece of goat cheese next to the biscuit made its Greek statement.

"It's nearly eleven!"

But I didn't care. I sipped and nibbled until the feast was done.

"You got to do right by your grandma, Mae. You got to strew them ashes on the river. But that ain't saying I don't worry about you out there by yourself." Stasia gazed at me as though trying to see through my eyeballs, past my skull, and right into my brain. She placed a hand on my shoulder.

"There's something fearful in you, Mae. I can feel it."

"Last night," I began and felt the cold river water wash over me. "I saw someone in the swamp, someone with a flashlight. He—if it was a he—shined it in the windows, then down there at the landing. When the light hit my boat, the person pulled back and went off into the swamp."

"You think he was looking for your boat?"

"Yes, and I think it's a Gruman. Not Toller who came to the funeral, but an old man I caught working bush hooks. I've seen him twice now."

"Sounds like Albert. He's old. Puts out bush hooks all over this river. Why would he be looking for your boat?"

"Meanness?" I shrugged.

"Revenge against Grandma?"

"Doubt it. Probably weren't a Gruman. Could be some swamp rat thought he could rob something here." Stasia laughed. "Man tried that once. Got a ark-full of Greeks on his back, yelling curses in English and Greek. Like to scared him to death. Nobody tried it since."

I lingered until noon when Stasia fed me leftovers gathered late last night from the wooden Sunday buffet tables. She caressed my shoulders, massaged my neck. We spoke little of the man in the woods, the Grumans, and Grandma. She told me instead of her births, of raising ten kids with no father but plenty of males in the extended family, and of her one trip back to the old country. "It's hard to call somewhere home that really isn't, Mae. I found myself in a squared-off white stone building, no glass or screens on the windows. The heat, humid as here, penetrated clear to the soul, not a tree anywhere to shade myself. We ate goat cheese and bread, drank strong tea and coffee. The old men had rotten teeth, what little teeth they had at all, and the old women wore solid black. I sat on a stool up on a hill and watched the young men push around the goats then go off to a church school. When the heat got too much, I moved inside the house where the sun didn't hit me and turn me dark as an African. If I sat just in the right spot, I could see the ocean, all blue and calm, and you know what? I thought of this river right here and I wanted to go home. Even in the evenings when we sat out back with some other relatives and drank strong wine while the men danced to the radio, even then I wanted to come home—here in this Southern swamp where our men go off to gather oysters and shrimp and mullet from the ocean. I spoke Greek there, but it didn't come off my tongue just right. When time came to dance the last round, I bid my farewells and vowed to write. Under my breath, I said so-long forever to the place where I was born. My soul belongs here, right here."

Stasia sat silent for a moment, her eyes staring somewhere far from the kitchen. "No, not even a tiny feeling for that Greek island," she said as though answering an invisible spirit who queried her.

"I have to go, Stasia," I said and placed the lunch dishes in the sink. "This is the last night I can spend on the river. I want to strew all the ashes by tomorrow morning."

"Where will you sleep tonight?"

"I'm not sure, but there are some places up the river, some houses of people I knew when I lived here. Most came to the funeral and know I'm depositing Grandma."

"The Gruman place isn't too far from the Bay Bridge. Keep your eyes peeled." Stasia squeezed me, then handed me a package of thick Greek bread and some cheese. "You'll be fine, Mae."

I watched this dame of all seasons stand on her screen porch and wave a stout arm, watched until I rounded a turn and could no longer see her. Then I felt a great loss. Like a child who sees a grandparent age, then drift away, I knew the protection of this powerful woman, just like Grandma, wouldn't be there forever.

I steered the boat through the lane, back to the main part of the river. Water birds called through the trees, announcing human arrival in the primeval forest. The sun faded about the time I turned into the deep water, and white clouds fluffed in the sky. I prayed for no rain, but in North Florida, this is a futile prayer. When the thunder roared loud enough to threaten lightning strikes, I looked for refuge. The first flash seemed to engulf the water and I thought I might meet God too soon.

Possibly thinking of God made me realize that the Church on the Bank had to be close. I had been there a few times as a child when Aunt Becky thought she might like a more progressive place than the Primitive Baptist. I turned on the motor and braved two more flashes before pulling up beside the remnants of a landing. I tied up, grabbed Grandma, and slipped upwards through mud and grass.

At the top of the bank, I could barely see the white wood-frame building through the thick oaks. Splashing mud up and down my legs, I dashed to the chipped stone steps. At first, I was sure the door was locked but a shove opened it a crack, and I knew it was only warped—a swamp hazard. As soon as I stepped inside, I felt the pressure of old smells. Swamp mildew combined with the natural wood in the pews and the dampened red carpet.

It reeked of funeral.

I pushed the door shut to keep out the rain that was now flooding everything, a blinding downpour. I shivered, then sat on a back pew and swiped at my wet arms and face. Digging a plastic tissue packet from my jeans pocket, I dried off as best I could. When I went for my feet, I saw my muddy footprints on the thin carpet. The carpet itself lay bare in spots, but especially in the center where endless congregations had trod to their favorite seats. My eyes followed the carpet to the pulpit, a once-white affair that allowed a male of anointed authority to tell females they should remain pure, to avoid fornication. I never understood that. If males weren't supposed to avoid fornication, and females must, then who would the males do it with? I started to laugh out loud at my silly thoughts when a tremendous clash of thunder and lightning sounded out of the heavens.

My hair stood on end—as I imagine did the man's who suddenly sat up straight in the front pew. We had to be forty feet from each other, and caddy-corned, but like two ghosts we stared in fright. He must have been lying there, maybe asleep. His hair, long and tangled and black, hung to his shoulders. It was hard to tell where his beard left off and his head hair began. Dressed in a ragged green jacket with a sweater underneath, he seemed to have no sense of the heat of the day. His eyes, however, pulled me in and I was reminded of the evil Rasputin. We said nothing, both realizing we were only here to escape the rain, but trusting no one. We had no reason to talk. I began to tremble inside, to shake against the dampness of the church and the molding wood of the pew.

Lightning struck somewhere hard again and again. Each time, we jumped and looked about as though the bolt would come through the locked windows. Two windows were stained-glass, setting off a yellow glow inside the church every time the lightning flashed. I couldn't say how long we sat there, looking, almost never blinking, but as the rain slackened, I watched the man's head lower slightly. The black eyes kept focused on me, however, and as they peered from beneath heavy black brows, he became increasingly sinister. When I heard thunder in the distance, and the windows no longer lit up with a flash, I darted from the pew, pulled on the door with both hands and headed for the swamp.

At the top of the bank, I realized Grandma was still there, sitting on a back pew in a sinister church with Rasputin at the front. I had no choice. Turning, I headed back and ran right into the beard and hair. Up close, the beard showed streaks of gray and the dark eyes sat deep inside gullies of crows-feet.

"This yours, lady?" The man's filthy hands gripped the urn at its widest section. He held it toward me.

"Yes, thank you," I said. I pulled the urn close to my body.

"Somebody you know?" The man shifted his jacket and closed the top button.

"My grandmother, yes, thank you." I moved backward, turning to see where I stepped.

"Good, that's good. Keep her with you. Grandmothers are good things. I remember one." He moved toward me a step or two. I smelled foul mouth odor mixed with cheap liquor.

"I'm sure you had a very nice grandmother." I half-slid to the boat and tucked the urn into the bottom. The man stayed at the top and stared down at me. "Ha!" he suddenly yelled. "Damn woman nearly killed me. Taught me how to drink then kicked me out of the house." He laughed then slid toward me before I could shove off. "You got something to eat in that boat?"

I grabbed Stasia's package. "Wonderful bread and cheese," I said and placed it on a patch of grass.

"Enjoy it."

"I do thank you, Miss Mae, and here's to your grandma, Miz Pope." The man grinned and bobbed his head at my disbelief.

"You know me?"

"Me and my brother painted your grandma's porch a long time ago. You was just a young lady then. You growed up real good, Mae, yessirree!"

"Your brother? What's your name?"

"Langford Richards, ma'am. Brother was Truman. We lived down by the old saw mill." Langford dug into the goat cheese, breaking off bits and shoving them through the massive hairs on his face.

"Where is Truman now?"

"Nam killed him. I didn't go. Too young. Army sent me to Germany later. That's where I got my soul all messed up." Langford let out a laugh and pulled out one of the pita breads. He held it up to the light then nibbled on it like it was a carrot stick.

"You mean drugs?" I'd heard of servicemen unable to cope, getting hooked on drugs, bringing back diseases.

"Gets me through the night, Miz Mae." He held the pita between his teeth, his beard surrounding it like a herd of black spiders, and thrust his fingers into his pocket. "You want to join me?" He showed me a joint, self-rolled and partially smoked.

"I don't smoke, Langford, never have."

"You and me could have some good laughs." I watched him set the food on a rotten log and light the smoke. He sipped in the drug as though he had a terrible thirst.

"Langford, do you know the Gruman family?"

He stopped and held the joint a few inches from his face. His eyes focused as best they could on me. If he didn't move soon, I was afraid the joint would set his beard on fire. "Know of them. Don't care to know them any better. Why? They around here some place?" He darted his eyes about without moving his head, then pulled another drag on the joint. It had burned nearly to his fingers.

"Not that I know of," I said. "Just wondered if they ever gave you any trouble."

"Never gave me anything else, Mae. And you stay away from them. They ain't nice to girls."

I nodded. Langford dropped to the ground, sitting in the mud. He poked at the food and tried to find more solace in the dying joint. His eyes no longer gazed down at me, but closed half-way then squinted at the sun.

"Don't talk to the painters, Mae. You'll distract them and they'll take twice as long to get done." Grandma jerked my arm and pulled me into the house. She had told me nearly four times to stay out of the way.

I liked the two fellows, their glossy black hair swept back like Elvis. Their black eyes danced when they teased me about my pretty red hair that kinked around my neck. The younger one winked and drew hearts on the wall with the white paint. When Grandma came to see, he quickly smeared it over and turned serious. She watched too much, I thought. The boys did a good job, covered every old board, even painted the swing like she said. But Grandma would stand just inside the screen door, her arms folded like a Samurai warrior. I wondered why she stared mostly at me and not the painters, but then they weren't right out there in her line of vision.

The last day, the brothers went to the side of the house to clean the brushes and pack up the paint buckets. I followed them, offering to rinse the brushes in the pungent turpentine. When the older one had replaced the lids, he said he needed help carrying them to the pickup truck. I volunteered.

Langford stayed behind, but he winked at me and his brother as we headed through the trees. I held two buckets, their weight pulling on my thin arms, then passed them to Truman to load. "You're a cute thing," he said. "Bet the boys after you all the time."

I blushed and felt the first thrill of male attention. When all the buckets had been carried to the truck and loaded, Truman reached down and squeezed my cheeks. "You a little older and I'd be after you good!"

A strange warmth rushed over my body, then just as quickly a chill followed. Grandma stood at the front of the truck. She had Joe's belt in her hand, the one he kept at Grandma's house along with the Sunday suit he changed into from his overalls.

"Your brother has your money. Now both of you vacate this property." Her voice sounded raspy, almost like she had a cold, only it didn't sound sick. She doubled the belt, then tapped her other hand with the folded part.

I knew the signal; I turned and ran. At the steps, I stopped and looked at the teenage Langford. He didn't wink, didn't even smile. The terror of unfriendliness engulfed me.

I spent the night touching my face, pretending it was Truman's hands on my cheeks. I relived his winks and heard his words until they faded and I let myself weep. Grandma killed feeling. No boy had ever squeezed her cheeks. I dreamed of Truman Richards for weeks until one Sunday we got an invitation to the Newman farm for an evening fish fry. People from miles would be there to eat bream and catfish, coated in cornmeal, fried in an outdoor cauldron.

Old man Newman kept a shed just for these occasions. The men would gather at a table several yards away to scale, gut, and filet the fish. Newman himself supervised the fish frying. Women, mostly his daughters and their cousins, stirred pots of grits or dropped balls of cornmeal, onion, and water into another cauldron of hot grease to make hush puppies. Women would bring gallons of iced tea for everyone. Some of the men kept six packs and whiskey jars in their trucks. Grandma, Uncle Nast, Aunt Becky, and I arrived at dusk. Old Joe, as usual for a social gathering, made himself scarce. The odor of frying fish permeated the forest. Some elderly people already sat in folding chairs or at a wooden table, pushing the fish meat off the bones and gumming the white flesh. They swallowed buttered grits with no trouble.

With the eating in full swing, drinking on the sly picked up with frequent visits to truck cabs. Adults, mellowed and sitting wherever they could, ignored us. I had nosed around Truman Richards all evening, bringing him tea and extra hush puppies. He laughed, chucked my chin, then looked off toward a plump towhead at least five years older than me. I didn't know her, but I didn't think she ought to be wearing thick red lipstick. She looked fat, and her dress stretched too tight over her front.

Once, I got into a game of chase with a boy from my school, then we expanded it into hide and seek. When I was "it," I found him behind a sticky palmetto bush. "Let's hide from the rest of them," he said, and moved closer to me. Scrawny and fresh-faced, he wasn't yet a man, but he had been learning their ways. "I like your red hair," he said. He let his small hand brush my braids. "I bet it looks real nice when you take it down."

I didn't know how to answer this. It felt good, but Grandma wouldn't have it, and I heard her in my head. "Don't let that boy touch your hair like that, Mae."

I ran into the woods. Some of the bigger kids giggled and screamed among the trees. I wanted to see what they were doing. I dodged underbrush and kissing couples until I saw Truman in a clearing. He had that fat, blond girl up next to him. They stood upright and danced, their bodies below the waist plastered together and moving in rhythm to distant music coming from a car radio. I hid behind a bush and watched. He stopped moving and backed the girl up to a tree. With one hand, he unbuttoned her tight dress. I stared at her face. Why didn't she scream for her grandma?

She glowed with a kind of embarrassed smile, and gripped the tree trunk behind her with both hands. This made her front push outward even more. Something stirred beside me. The kid had followed me from my hiding spot.

"You spying on them?" he said and moved close enough to touch my shoulder.

I shook my head. When I looked back, Truman had completely undone the dress front and was reaching inside to unhook her bra. With a little help from him, her breasts unfolded and plopped forward into his palms.

I gasped. As Truman leaned over to touch the girl's tits with his lips, my child's game companion put his hand on my chest and began to unbutton my shirt. I froze. Not in disbelief or shame, but in the horror that when he got down to flesh, nothing was going to unfold. I didn't look much different from a boy in that area.

The kid never got to the third button. A voice and a swipe came from the darkness like a hellish demon. "Get your filthy fingers away from her!" Grandma lifted a broom and whacked at the kid, spanking him as he tried to dart out of the thick undergrowth. "I'll chop them off if I catch you doing that again!" She chased after him like a witch, full of whiskey and swinging a broom.

Truman Richards disappointed me. I hated him for kissing that girl, but late at night, I would put myself in her place and feel the warm lips on my nonexistent breasts.

"I'm sorry to hear about Truman in Nam. You take it easy, Langford." I reached the safety of the open river. After putting distance between me and Langford, I eased the throttle and pulled up next to a cypress where I yanked down a strand of moss. Carefully, I wiped the mud and fingerprints off the urn. Nearby, a family of turtles moved off a log, falling into the water one at a time. Fresh steam rose from the cool river now that the rain had passed and the sun turned the spot into a greenhouse. Beyond the rays, however, more clouds gathered. There would be rain during the night.

XI

I reached the Bay Bridge at twilight. The clouds had lingered in the distance, their bursts less of a threat now. I stopped beneath the bridge to allow the damp shade to cool me down from the afternoon rays. Overhead, the occasional thump of car tires hit the bridge, then moved to the highway and disappeared into the trees. A few had turned on their lights. On both sides of the bridge, dirt ruts ran from the road to the river where people parked their boat trailers at water's edge. This time of evening, the ruts were deserted except for a battered truck that read "Mannie's Repair" on the door.

A young man, maybe no more than twenty-five, leaned against one side. He smoked cigarettes, taking one out of a package, waiting to finish the first one. When a small red car pulled off the road and came to a stop behind the truck, the man tossed his cigarette into the river and opened the car door. "Any problems?" The man, in spite of his youth, had a bass voice.

"Thought he'd never get out of the house. He's gone to play poker; we can take our time." A woman who looked to be in her teens, her bleached blond hair threatening to touch her tiny waist, clung to the man. She turned to him, and as they headed to the base of the bridge, unbuttoned his shirt. I eased the boat into a shadow while the couple tossed down an Army blanket just under the abutment. Within seconds, they had each other undressed and fondled. When the man entered her, the blond whimpered and squealed, her buttocks jumping about beneath the man's narrow hips. He made no sound, but moved ferociously, claiming what he could never really have.

I thought of moving to the other side of the river, or going back up a few yards. Either way, I would have been seen, would have disturbed the basic pleasure of two people who had to seek out shadows. A car pulled slowly over the bridge. It had turned onto the ruts before I could see where it headed. In the encroaching darkness, I saw the brown and white of a sheriff's marked car. It came to a stop behind the red car, and a large man emerged. He did not wear a uniform. Reaching into my bag inside the boat, I pulled out a flashlight. Waving the beam at the couple, I finally caught the attention of the girl. She slid like a fish from under the man, gasping and grabbing at her clothes.

"Damn, Sally!" said the man as he grabbed his erection.

"Someone's looking," she said.

I ran the light up the bank, warning them of the danger above.

"Sally!" The man from the sheriff's car stood with his hands on his hips, his voice demanding an answer.

"Damn! It's Harold. Get out of here. That way!" Sally pointed to the river.

Her lover scooped up his clothes and slid to the water. Just before he went in, I flashed the light again.

"Get in the boat," I said, and wondered why. I pushed from under the bridge. The man sunk down underneath my bundled sleeping bag. The people on shore wouldn't notice us in the dark, but we could hear them.

The man cursed and called for Sally to get her butt back to her car. Sally, in a calm voice, said she'd just come to catch the moonlight on the water. She must have put on her clothes by then.

I turned a bend and pulled next to a newly built landing where an expensive fishing boat tied up. "Get out here. You'll have to walk back to your truck, but you'd better wait about an hour."

The man nodded, but all I could see was shadow moving. Then I felt him grab hold of the ladder on the landing. The boat swayed as he pulled himself out. "Thanks, lady," he whispered before he disappeared into the swamp.

Scenes of revenge jumped through my brain. Sally, her pretty face bruised and broken, her lover's truck engine smashed beyond repair. The lessons of adultery never took hold like the lessons of brutish retribution. Clouds moved closer.

I had to find a place to put ashore. Another abandoned fish cleaning station sat in a small cove near the bridge. If I could find it, I would face my fears and set up the sleeping bag out of the rain. The river lane to the cove had overgrown with oak limbs. I had to shove them aside and ride stooped over to reach the open-sided shed. Nearly dark now, I used the flashlight to pull the boat into the bank grass and lay the bag on the ground. I opened the cooler and pulled out stale ham and cornbread, and longed for the pita and goat cheese that Langford had washed down with marijuana.

The clouds moved, opening a crack every now and then for a full moon to dash some light on my surroundings. I ate, shoved the wrappers back into the boat and pulled Grandma on shore with me. I lay on the ground, the tufts of grass pressing into my back, and stared at the rusted tin roof. Fish had been gutted by the hundreds right where I lay. I closed my eyes, hearing the cry of catfish and bass as their bodies ripped apart.

I sat up. The cries were real. A female voice, in the distance and coming closer, called out, "Stop it! Toller, Stop it!"

Movement ceased and the voice just cried, loud like a child who had been whipped. I crept through the brush that pulled at my clothes. In a clearing near the river, a man shoved his body over a young girl. I first saw the white of his uncovered buttocks, then the terrified eyes of the girl. A single wailing sound emanated from her mouth, unceasing.

Toller held her wrists in the mud, forcing her to lie still. My body shook, and outrage overtook fear. Running back to the boat, I grabbed an oar. I didn't say anything to the couple, just lifted the oar back and brought it down on Toller's head. He looked up at me, eyes dazed from sex and a head injury. When he rolled off the girl, he tumbled backward and came to lay face down in the mud, his thinning hair wet with river water.

The girl never saw me. Her face had been turned the other way. Freed from her pain, she leapt into the forest and ran, bellowing like haints were chasing her. I stood over Toller. He moaned once and twitched. I started to kneel toward him, when a voice came from the trees.

"Don't touch him! Help me." Old Joe appeared from the other side of the swamp, his overall buttons shining in the moonlight. With his good side, he pulled on Toller's shoulder. "Get the other one."

I grabbed hold of the man's heavy upper arm. We pulled him to the river until his head dropped under the water.

"Now help me shove him," Joe said after he saw Toller wasn't going to save himself. We pushed on his heavy legs. In minutes, he had disappeared. "River cave starts right here. He won't be found." Old Joe looked at me. I stared back, shaking and following orders. "Now get on down the river and take that oar with you. Go to the brackish water. You ain't never seen nor done nothing. You hear?"

I nodded. Joe broke a tree branch and wiped the mud where Toller's body had slid into the water. He used his right arm, dragging the useless left side like chains he couldn't remove. "Rain will wash all this away before dawn. Now, git!" He glared at me, like Grandma did when she had told me twice to do something.

I backed into the trees. The oar, the sleeping bag, Grandma, all fell into the boat with me. My trembling hands couldn't get the motor to start, then some guiding spirit made me stop and think. The sound could attract anyone in the forest. I used the oar to push off and propel me into the main part of the river. In the process, the already damaged thing broke, its paddle dropping into the water grass. Holding the broken handle in my hand, I remembered Old Joe and began to hand paddle the water. It got me into the center of the river.

Sometime after I had turned on the motor, I felt the rain on my face. Mixing with salty tears, it ran down my cheeks and fell onto my chest. I dropped the broken oar handle overboard. Water covered my heart, flowed over it like the river, and the currents hurt.

XII

The manatee's cow-like body formed a shadow just below the surface. It made sluggish turns, dipping, then stretching its body folds, ignoring the lowering of my engine just above its head. Signs warned to slow or turn off motors in the area. Manatees down below could be slashed and bloody the water. They are endangered because they live close to harm and aren't smart enough to dodge it. The river here widened like a huge broken pipe. If I traveled a few more miles, I would hit ocean and breathe in the antiseptic odor of salt. Instead, I pulled into a landing area not far from a dock. In the distance, I saw lights on luxury boats tied up next to slips owned by rich people. Their rich houses sat back from the landings, shining outdoor lights off latticed balconies.

I wouldn't go that far. I preferred the shadows of a canopied cove. The rain slackened for a while but I didn't care. I slipped to the floor of the boat, my sleeping bag unfolded underneath me. It was wet just like me. I lay back with my eyes closed and let the drizzle hit my arms and face. Later, showers drenched me, but I welcomed the cold drops, the heavenly bath. At dawn, the new sun dried my face, leaving my skin parched and burning.

When I watched the last of Grandma's ashes drop into the eddy, I took the urn and rinsed it over the side. Thinking again, I lifted the urn over the side and let go. It filled and sank. I threw in the lid. "Now, Grandma, you are home. And, guess what? Little Miss Alligator really did clobber that old bull over the head with an oar, didn't she?"

Carefree voices and laughter sounded in the distance. The rich people emerged from their private homes to their private docks, carrying expensive rods that would haul in mighty swordfish who hadn't yet evolved enough to stop grabbing hold of the fish bait on heavy sea hooks.

Monday, the final day of my river journey, the sun slammed into me like a ray gun. I lifted my bruised body off the soaked sleeping bag and managed to sit where I could turn on the motor. For a moment, I didn't know where to go, then I remembered Aunt Becky and Uncle Nast were to meet me back at the fork around noon. Was it only last Friday that arrangement had been made? I turned the boat around with my hands, facing inland from where I came, and turned on the motor.

As soon as I cleared the manatee habitat, I revved the motor full throttle. In less than two hours, I covered the miles it had taken me three days to descend. I passed a few boats, slowing for safety and courtesy, then revving high again. Soon I skimmed along the river, a wake of equal tracks of water following behind. My face took the spray and thanked the heavens for it. I passed under Bay Bridge at high speed, never glimpsing toward the lane that would take me to the abandoned fish cleaning shed. Without looking, I sensed when I shot past the Church by the Bank, then, like a backward camera, I passed Stasia's water lane, the Ageless Hippies' camp site, and finally the first group of fish sheds. I began to slow and saw the last of the bush hooks, their yellow and orange ties standing up like warnings of encroaching dangers to nature itself.

The fork lay in front of me. When I turned off St. Margaret's, the water narrowed, but the noise grew. The state had built a landing here, an elaborate affair with slanted pavement into the water and a cement parking lot for cars and their boat trailers. Public toilets sat at the end of the lot inside a cement block structure painted brown. Between the Women's and the Men's, a lone water fountain collected dust, waiting for the next thirsty child to step on a cement block and squirt lukewarm, sulfur-tinted water into his mouth.

I pulled to a side slip made especially for small motorboats. Aunt Becky and Uncle Nast got out of their car the moment they saw me. "You look a mess!" said Aunt Becky and held her arms wide open for me to hug her. "But you did it, didn't you?"

Uncle Nast didn't say anything, just nodded and grinned and shook my hand. "I'll drive the car around and pull out the boat for you." He wiped his eyes under his glasses as soon as he turned his back.

"He's really proud, Mae, and sure happy that you laid his mama to rest where she wanted to be. He ain't gonna say it, but he's mighty proud."

"Yes," I said, weary enough to feel my bones ache. "You got the air-conditioning on in the car?"

"Of course. That's where we were sitting, waiting for you." Aunt Becky moved close and took a frowning look at my neck. "You got skeeter bites, Mae. Bet they're all over your legs. Them things always get me on my legs."

"I gave Miz Stasia the pound cake. She said thank you." I felt if I kept talking I could shake the feeling that people stared at me.

"She doing okay?" Aunt Becky didn't wait for an answer. "Don't know how that woman lives out there in them woods like that. It ain't nice to my way of thinking."

"Not nice?"

"I mean, she's got to be rugged-like, kill snakes and watch for gators, stuff no lady likes to do."

"Not all women are ladies, Aunt Becky, at least not the kind you hoped to be." I hadn't meant to be cruel. It's just that my aunt's superficial judgments smacked of no importance at the moment.

"Just like your grandma, Miss Mae, uppity about women living in the swamp and making it by themselves." She sighed. "But, I guess your grandma did make it. She was one fearless and brave woman."

I rested my head on the back of the car seat and closed my eyes. "Grandma might have been brave, but she wasn't fearless. She was scared half to death most of her life. And she didn't make it by herself. She had a gnarly-skinned green gator called Old Joe waiting in the wings to rescue her from just about anything." I leaned my head against the window and pretended to sleep. Uncle Nast settled in the driver's seat.

"She looks tired," he said and started the car.

"Poor thing," said Aunt Becky. "Turn up the air, will you?"

I spent the evening wrapped in Aunt Becky's care and her home-quilted coverlet. Shivers took over me once as I lay on the guest bed. Aunt Becky had arranged it to display her tatting talents. Lace doilies graced everything, including the window sills where she had fastened them carefully with a transparent-headed tack. Atop the sleigh headboard, she placed a huge round one with two small ones on either side. They looked like Jesus and the two thieves on their crosses, and I wondered if I stared long enough would Jesus forgive me, too.

I dozed. Voices nudged me once in a while, and I pictured the mosquito women from the church, whispering and glancing at me, quietly accusing me of doing the world a favor but trying to hide it. I ran behind a palmetto bush and peed on my bare feet. The women wouldn't find me there, and they wouldn't want to touch me if they did.

"She's tired, Bobby. I don't know if she can talk right now."

My eyes opened to the darkened room. Foot steps sounded outside my door.

"She's got to be told. You want to get her up?"

The door opened. Aunt Becky's profile stood in the hall light like a heavenly ghost come to toss me to hell.

"Mae, wake up. It's Bobby Thompson, the deputy sheriff. He wants you to know something 'cause he thinks you'd be in charge. You got to get up and listen to him." She watched me stare up at her, then clasped both hands over her mouth.

"Are you ill, Aunt Becky?" I sat up. I could see Bobby and Uncle Nast peering in from the hall.

"Oh, sweetie, it's Old Joe. They found him on his porch this afternoon. Seems he had that final stroke."

I shivered again, then asked for light. Aunt Becky opened the blinds. The fading western sun cast an eerie glow in the room.

"Did he die alone?"

Bobby came into the room. His uniform, starched and bearing the department star, seemed to enter before he did.

"Yeah, Mae. Old man Skipper Lou found him sprawled on the porch. Never had a chance, I guess."

Uncle Nast's mouth hung open and silent. His long face had paled and he swiped it in a downward motion like he wanted to rid himself of the folded skin. He paced like a sentinel outside my door.

"Who is his next of kin?"

"You got to be it, Mae, and your Uncle Nast here. He don't have a family that I know of. You two and your grandma was about all he had. Anyhow, sheriff said to get hold of you for arrangements soon as the coroner finishes."

"Is tomorrow too soon?" Bobby reached down and placed a huge hand on my shoulder. The warmth ran through me and the tremors stopped. I'd had a crush on Bobby Thompson when I was in tenth grade. He played ball rough, but he was a gentle giant to the girls. I smelled his Old English aftershave and bet he'd been using it for over thirty years.

"I can come get you," he turned first to me, then to Uncle Nast, "take you to the morgue."

Aunt Becky gasped and ran from the room. Uncle Nast stared, his face ashen, but made no move to run after her. I took hold of Bobby's wrist to balance myself. "If that's what I have to do, yes. Pick me up. Uncle Nast doesn't have to go."

I slept, but Gruman men and screaming children and rain flooding the boat kept slapping me and waking me. I finally crawled out from under the handmade quilt. My throat on fire, I had a thirst like I'd been on the desert for a week. In Aunt Becky's kitchen I touched the fruit pottery that held flour, sugar, and cornmeal. Each one—a strawberry, a peach, a melon—was lidded with the stem or leaf design of the fruit. Over the sink, yellow dotted-swiss curtains barely blocked the porch light. I filled up a plastic glass left over from the fifties, pushed back the curtain, and watched the rain while I drank.

Here I was in Aunt Becky's and Uncle Nast's house, where I lived, then went out to school, the doctor, to church, and to Grandma's on Sundays, but why wasn't I comfortable here? I shuddered inside like a prisoner in a cold jail and wondered if that's where I'd end up. Old Joe wouldn't be telling. There was that girl, the one Toller was raping. I didn't think she saw me, but in my mind she pointed straight to my face and let out that wail like a stabbed cow. The sound never left me.

The rain pounded into the edges of Uncle Nast's attempt at a lawn, causing the dirt edges to expand into mud then run the length of the yard. When it widened, it disturbed a frog that jumped into the road to avoid being caught in the flood. I watched it hop until the light faded.

"Little Miss Alligator had to run once, Mae. Got herself stuck in the mud down near the shore. She'd been down there bathing, just a frolicking in that clear spring water, her green skin hanging on a tree." Grandma eyed me sadly. "Didn't you know she could take off her suit, especially when the weather was hot?"

I started to giggle, but Grandma frowned, then her eyes got the most painful look I've seen ever. I made myself serious and waited for the next sentence.

"Well, like I said, she were swimming round in this clear water, when up on the shore this mean old bull gator reared its knotty head and showed its bank of white teeth and dared her to come out of the water." Grandma stared away, her Mason jar nearly tilting over in her lap. "But she knew better. Wouldn't come out and expose herself no matter what." She lifted the jar and took a long drag.

"What happened, Grandma?" I whispered this as I knew Grandma had found an anger somewhere and it could use me as the butt as sure as the day had sunshine.

"Don't hurry me, Mae." She took another swig. Her eyes looked bleary and tired. "Go shake that man." She pointed to Joe who snored and snorted from the swing.

I sat in the swing next to Joe without touching him. Maybe he felt my presence, because his breathing became lighter and the snoring ceased.

"Okay, Grandma," I whispered from her side.

"Little Miss Alligator couldn't stay in that water forever, even if that is where she came from." Grandma spoke easily now, maybe because she could talk to the outdoors and not see me. "She had to find a way out soon. The old bull, of course, couldn't stay out of the water forever, either, but he could stay out a lot longer than she could stay in." Grandma stopped as though computing what she had just said, hoping it made sense. "If she darted out, he'd surely get her in that ugly mouth of his. If she stayed in, he'd come in after her and she'd go down his throat alongside tadpoles, frogs, and maybe a few fish if bull gator was lucky." Grandma stopped again. She still looked far out over the river like she wanted to see something over the other side, only I thought the other side was more like the past.

"Did she get out?"

"You see her up and about, don't you?"

My head felt jarred. Grandma had never told me she could actually see Little Miss Alligator. Maybe that's why she looked off over the river every time she sat on the front porch.

"No, ma'am, I don't see her."

Grandma remained silent for too many minutes then she pulled back to herself and smiled down at me. Running her fingers through my hair, she said, "Yeah, Mae, you do. You'll know it someday, too." Grandma puzzled me then left me to pull off into that gaze again.

"Did she get out, Grandma? Little Miss Alligator, how did she get out of the river?"

"Darted down a ways, jumped out and ran lickety-split into the swamp. She found a place, an old cave whose opening had nearly closed up with rock and mud. She hid there for hours, listening to the old bull snort and call after her not far away. When he finally had to go back into the water, she slipped out, snatched her gator hide off the limb and high-tailed it out of that

River Whispers

swamp."

"Where did she run, Grandma?" Grandma looked down at me, her eyes watering. Then she smiled a huge grin. Some of the water ran out of her eyes. "You really been following me, haven't you?"

I nodded, but a knot grew in my throat. I was convinced that Grandma was going to kill off Little Miss Alligator with this story.

"Yeah, Mae, she got away," she said almost matter of factly. "She's still in the swamp, you know. So's Mr. Bull Alligator, and she has to keep a close watch out for him. She's a big gator now with a lot of know-how, but she don't trust them reptiles. She's got her friends. They keep her in the know."

"Friends kept you in the know, didn't they, Grandma?" I lifted the glass in a toast to the frog that escaped a mud drowning. I drank until the liquid ran down the corners of my mouth and landed on my nightgown. Then I toasted once more. "Here's to you, Old Joe. Tell Grandma hello."

I cried that night, kept the drizzling rain company as it landed on the roof. I awoke to the odor of fresh biscuits and frying bacon. For a moment, in the quiet and warmth of my room, under a home-sewn quilt, I thought I might be back in Grandma's house, in the little room where she kept a bed for me. It might have been a closet, or better, some kind of alcove, but she stuck a cot there with a tiny table and lamp next to it. It came to be known as Mae's room. I treated it more like a sanctuary. Stuck in the back of the house, it provided the privacy that a young girl needs.

During the day, I stored my comic books along with my movie star cutouts underneath the cot. I'd read all the Hollywood magazines and cut out the pictures of my favorites: Mario Lanza, Doris Day, and George Nader. When I found out I could, I wrote letters to them in care of Hollywood, California, to ask for a signed photograph. I always got one. The perfect faces on Susan Hayward and Linda Darnelle, their fancy signatures scrawled across their shoulders, stacked up until Uncle Nast bought me a scrapbook to paste them in with white glue.

It lived in Grandma's house, along with the framed photo of Robert Wagner who had just about the most perfect face and body of any man I had ever seen. I figured if I could meet him, he'd fall in love with me and take care of me forever. He'd smile all the time, just like in the picture, and bring home lots of movie money and build me a swimming pool. We didn't go to the movies much, but one time Aunt Becky insisted on Uncle Nast taking us to the drive-in to see "Titanic." That was my first view of Robert Wagner. I spent all my nights for years, dreaming of how I'd been on that ship and he had saved me. I grew up and met Jack.

I squeezed my eyes tight; a tear oozed from one. Jack and Robert Wagner! What was I thinking? A knock sounded at the door. "Mae, you got to get up. You said you needed to call your office, and Bobby's gonna be here in a little while. You awake yet?"

Inside the morgue, I got the impression of being engulfed in light green cement. No pictures graced the walls, only carefully placed lights that reminded us we still lived. Uncle Nast insisted on going with me, but he shuffled behind like an old dog who wanted to hunt but couldn't stand the taste of blood anymore.

"He's on that pull-out shelf," said Bobby, nearly whispering. "You just look at him through this window and identify him."

The coverlet, white and antiseptic, didn't belong on Old Joe. He needed Grandma's quilt, something with patches of color like the shadows in the swamp. And the thing was too thin. It revealed the profile of a man, gave him no dignity. The attendant pulled back the cover just above Old Joe's nipples, and I turned my head in shame. He never exposed himself in life. I'd never even seen him in a swimsuit.

"Mae," said Bobby who took hold of my arm, "you got to look."

I stared at the bruised face or at least it looked that way. One half was nearly purple. The silver brows shined like tinsel in the morgue light and I could see little spikes of beard which Joe hadn't shaved too well. Probably didn't shave at all that day. His lips caved inward without his dentures in place. He hated the things and rarely used them, only when he wanted to chew on meat. "Why is he dark on one side of his face?"

"He fell kind of head downwards; all the blood settled there. It looked like he had been sitting in his swing, got hit by the stroke and keeled over forward. He was on his knees with his head down in front, only turned to one side."

I heard a grunt from Uncle Nast and turned to see him wipe at his eyes and head for the door.

"It's Old Joe," I said for Bobby's record. "Do I get to bury him, too?"

"If you want to." I looked at Bobby, his gray eyes dog-like in their faithfulness. He had only strands of hair now, and a belly that spoke of Southern barbecue, but he still needed to be the hero for the little girls at school.

"I wouldn't let anyone else do it," I said.

XIII

"You aren't going down that river again, Mae!" Aunt Becky stood in the living room while I talked to the undertaker. Bobby, his uniform smelling of fresh detergent and hot iron, sat in a swivel rocker, looking uncomfortable, like he was marooned on a sand bar.

"I'm paying for the cremation, Aunt Becky. What I do with the ashes remains to be decided." I touched her arm. "Now let me do this."

Old Joe's bank account would pay for a modest funeral but he had no burial plot. Bobby said the county would do something about it, but I wouldn't dump him in a weedy grave with no marker. Joe needed to be with Grandma at the bottom of St. Margaret's River.

"Well, Mae," said Bobby, standing up and tugging at the tight shirt. I couldn't tell if the tightness was from a bullet-proof vest or a too-small size. "There's another matter I got to look into right now. Seems one of the Gruman men has gone missing. Probably a blessing on the swamp if he got tangled in a nest of moccasins, but I got to go nonetheless."

"I'll take care of Old Joe, and thanks, Bobby."

River Whispers

Bobby stood for a minute. His once Apollo-blond hair had thinned. Only a few strands on top blended in with his scalp. Sculpted jowls over strong cheek bones now sagged, rounding his face that rested on a roll of chin. His arms, fatty now, would still be strong, but he winced a little when he got out of the chair, like his knees were going. Once, I trembled in his presence, couldn't get out a single word when he asked if I could help him find a library book. He's less intimidating now. I think he trembles in my presence, just a little.

"Bobby Thompson got married!" The phrase hit the river and the town simultaneously. Depression and envy flattened all the girls who hoped for a hug from the Atlas-chested, flat-stomached angel. He'd run off the night of graduation with one of the graduating cheerleaders. When the two didn't come back after the all-night party, her parents ambushed his with shotguns.

I dreamed that night, of being the girl at the graduation party, the one who had vamped Bobby and led him astray. I wore a filmy white gown and hyacinth flowers in my hair. We ran through the swamp, Bobby carrying me in his strong arms over mud and rowing me down the river in a sparkling canoe. We left the swamp, the humidity, and lived in a castle by the shore. Awakening, I felt like people do when their dreams are good, calm, right with the day. I wasn't the girl that got him, but pretending made it almost true.

I met Bobby again when he came home from the army, heftier and sullen. He took a job with the sheriff's department, the only thing, he said, he was suited for, having tried selling clothes, running a gardening service, and repairing cars. His wife had cheered herself out of his life and married another enlisted man. Still a gentleman, he settled in, became a Southern middle-class bachelor and forever forgot his days as the football Adonis. For all his prettiness and male perfection, Bobby turned out just like all the girls' daddies—fat-bellied, balding, and humbled.

I rested next to Old Joe's boat at his tiny landing. The boat needed painting and the oars had cracked. A long push-pole lay length-wise across the slat seats, and a torn net on a rusted handle lay in the bottom. The landing itself, a few boards leading to a post in the water, no longer held the weight of a human. I sat flat on the sloping bank. Through my thin slacks I felt the dampness of grass that poked up from muddy earth. In my hands, I held a metallic box. Not the shiny brass urn I had for Grandma, but a simple box, dark steel, that reflected none of the morning sunlight. Inside, the man who waltzed me across a linoleum floor as gently as the prince waltzed Cinderella, lay in a crumble of fine ash and bone. Secrets in the box, silent, but beckoning to me like the misty ghosts on the river surface.

"Your grandma's broke her arm," Old Joe said over the pay phone. "I had to bring her up to the fork on the boat. One of Miz Stasia's boys going to carry her up to the Tallahassee hospital in his truck."

Joe never had a phone and thought he had to yell when he talked into one, like the twenty-mile distance needed some help.

At the hospital, Joe sat in the plastic waiting room chair, his cap hanging on one knee, his eyes cast downward. His overall bib still held three feathery fishhook flies. He'd explained that he had taken a mess of catfish to Grandma, found her lying on the porch where she had tripped on a rotten board. "Just lying there groaning, her arm swole up like she been snake bit. Scared me good, till she told me she fell." He had lifted her to the boat where he made her comfortable and rowed to the fork. "She wouldn't leave without that Mason jar, no sirreee!" He grinned, his broken teeth stained with wet snuff.

Grandma had to move in with Aunt Becky. She didn't know it then, but she would never live in her river house again.

"Rotted and termite-eat," said Uncle Nast on one of his rare visits to my apartment in Tallahassee. "It's got to be rebuilt or left to the elements."

"She's too old to live there alone." I made the pronouncement expected of me, but I felt the sting of shame. Grandma was made out of that river. An inland house would kill her.

"The river ghosts come out of that mist," she once said to me on a humid day after a rain when fog rose off the water and edged onto shore. "You be still enough, you'll hear them talk, tell tales about people who been up and down here, even about those who gone down and never come up. All you got to do is be still and listen." Then she stopped rocking, her eyes glazed over and focused somewhere near the center of the river. Thick mist engulfed the porch. The river had come to embrace us and pull us out where we'd never be seen again. I slid over and grabbed onto Grandma's shins, but she didn't move.

Grandma stayed with her broken arm and misplaced spirit in a brick house Uncle Nast had built. She slept in my old room, her body shrunken with age; she looked like a child in the single bed. Once in a while, Uncle Nast would find a way to get her to Old Joe's, where they spent Sunday afternoon. At twilight, she sipped a little from the jar and left him dozing in his swing.

I placed the box underneath the seat of Old Joe's boat, then shoved off with his pole. As soon as I reached deep water, I used an oar to guide the boat to the Skourous water lane. As I rounded the bend, I took the pole again and pushed the banks until I saw Stasia sitting on her old houseboat deck. She stood when she saw me, her heavy frame and gray hair like a beacon in a storm. She expected me.

"You got a plan?" Stasia had shooed off her grandchildren, sent them down the river to buy fish off the family boat.

"I'll strew them in the river with Grandma, of course."

"You plan on putting them in the same spots?" Stasia sipped her tea. She eyed me, her voice tense like she needed to ask more.

"No, I won't travel the river again. Maybe put them near Grandma's old place. He was happiest there."

"Was he?"

I looked at her. She stared at the river, her olive skin caught the sun's rays and suddenly revealed her seventy-plus years. I shuddered. Time would run out for this icon of my youth, too.

"He stayed there a lot." It was more a question than a proof of Old Joe's happiness.

"When your grandma got sick, had to move in with your Uncle Nast and Aunt Becky, Old Joe didn't keep up her place. He let it rot. Moved back to his house and kept it right nice."

I nodded. The boards never rotted, and he kept it painted. The sandy soil out front stayed raked. Sometimes he filled it in with topsoil and planted winter grass. Not that I visited it often. Old Joe's place, his sanctuary at the back of three acres that boarded on the river, remained private until the day he died in the porch swing.

"It's mine, now, Stasia. Lawyer said he willed it to Grandma and her descendants. Uncle Nast wants no part of it. He deeded it to me. I was wondering…" I looked at her bare feet, her wide hips stretching her jersey house dress. "Would you like to see it with me?"

"Long as you drive me. I ain't getting in that boat." She didn't laugh. Her agreement maybe meant it was a load she didn't really want to carry. I needed her to carry it anyway.

"You ladies hold on," said Bobby as he bounced his highrider swamp truck over ridges and between trees. "Used to be a rutted road back through here, but not too many people used it. Old Joe never encouraged visitors."

I sat squeezed between Bobby's solid frame and Stasia's soft one. She held the overhead handle and grunted each time a bounce shifted her weight to one side or the other. When we hit a hole with a thud, knocking all three of us in her direction, she uttered something in Greek. Bobby ran the airconditioner full blast, his aftershave permeating the cab.

When at last we could see Old Joe's house through the forest, we relaxed and took the final bumps with stoic relief. "Not a bad-looking place," said Bobby as he eased Stasia out of the high cab and onto a wooden stool he carried in the truck.

She wore plastic thongs, the kind you take showers in, on her feet. When her weight hit the stool on her right foot, the thong made a slapping sound just before she came down hard.

"Maybe I should have taken the boat after all." Stasia's forehead broke out in sweat, and she breathed heavily, leaning up against the truck while Bobby helped me slide off the seat.

"You got the boxes, Bobby?" I had asked him to bring some cardboard crates so we could gather Joe's clothes, maybe give them to the Salvation Army.

"In the truck," he said, and took the lead toward the front porch. "See right here," Bobby said, pointing to the worn boards just in front of the porch swing. "This is where he was when Skipper found him, kind of leaning over onto the side of his face. Sheriff said it looked like the stroke got him as he was about to stand up or it made him lurch forward enough to fall out, face first."

"No signs that someone pushed him, or tried to kill him?" I waited, praying Bobby wouldn't pick up on my trembling.

"Nope. Medical Examiner opened him up and found a massive stroke. He didn't linger like your Grandma." Bobby leaned over, his uniform creaking in places it wouldn't give. "Died right here." He tapped the floor.

Bobby left us to it. He roamed the property, pines and oaks packed onto overgrown bush-covered forest. I'd been over it earlier. From the house, the ground sloped toward the river, and Joe's lot narrowed. His landing and a few feet to each side was all he had of river front. The house itself sat under an enormous oak, its branches loaded with moss. From the porch, you couldn't see the river, might not know there was one if you didn't know the woods. Stasia eased herself into a straight-back dining chair and fanned with a fishing magazine she found on the wooden table. The table itself was chipped, the dark stain revealing natural oak beneath. It had room for six, but Joe's other chairs were placed about the living room, and one in the bedroom.

One's living quarters, especially after fifty years, reveal accumulated experiences, what one has become in total, instead of distinct periods of history. Joe sat in upright chairs. The worn sofa, covered with a frayed chenille bedspread, held a plastic box of medicine bottles, more magazines on fishing, and his tackle box. I pictured him pulling the hooks from the box, his left hand shaking as he forced it to act with the right one to attach the line. He would shove off the landing, move out a few yards to deeper water, and cast his line. He'd sit in the boat for hours, maybe sleeping, maybe thinking of younger days with Grandma, and pulling in a catfish for the night's supper.

"Looks like he kept the frying pan ready," said Stasia, cooled down and going through the tiny kitchen. "Don't know how he moved around in here."

"There's a walking stick in every room," I said as I picked up one from the living area, then found another in the kitchen.

"He weren't well, Mae. He needed the stick." Stasia pressed one hand on her hip. "And if I ride in that truck too much longer, I'm going to need one."

We opened cabinets. Joe's dishes, some chipped china, some functional plastic, sat alongside teal blue and maroon-colored aluminum glasses. He kept large mugs and a shelf of unopened coffee cans. On the stove, the iron skillet sat cleaned, ready to accept the meal of the day. On another burner, Joe kept an old-fashioned coffee percolator.

"Got the basics in the fridge—bologna, bread, and mayonnaise. And, a box of oranges on the floor." Stasia closed the refrigerator door. "You got somebody to take this stuff out of here?"

I didn't. I'd have to do it myself, but right now, I looked for other things. She followed me to the bedroom. The basic twin bed with a quilt I'm sure Grandma gave him, two end tables with bright-bulbed lamps, a chest of drawers—they were what anyone would find in a loner's room.

"Here's his suit," I said as I opened the closet. "The one he wore to the funeral." One heavy overcoat hung beside the suit. The rest of the closet held boxes, yellowed, their paper contents sticking from bulges at the corners. We pulled out photos, young men and women of the river, and knew no one. In some the women stood near the river in full-length dresses, their bodies covered up to their chins and down to their wrists.

"Bet these ladies died of sweat," said Stasia. She placed the photos in neat stacks on the dining table. "Why didn't that old man put names on the backs?"

"I never knew he had a camera," I said, staring at a faded black-and-white image of a newly built river house that looked a lot like my grandmother's. Like the ruins of Pompey, the deeper one digs, the more one finds. Below the photo boxes, yellowed copies of the local papers from the forties appeared. Some told of the war's end, of local tragedies when soldiers ran the beach at Normandy, and those who came home whole, ready to plant watermelon, corn, and peanuts. There in the stack, a group of papers spoke of excessive summer rains, the swelling river, ruined oyster beds, and the disappearance of Artimus Gruman, a local fisherman.

"They searched the swamp, it seems." I passed the crumbling paper to Stasia. "Used some hunting dogs, too."

"I remember," she said, glancing at the paper then putting it aside as though unworthy of her study. "Wasn't much of a law force back then, but what there was looked all over. Bet you'll find in one of those papers that they finally figured he fell in the river or a sink hole and drowned. They won't tell you how much he drank, how nasty he got. But we all knew it was just as possible for him to fall foul of his own nature as to be bashed in the head by somebody who hated his guts." Stasia's black eyes flared at me, showing the determination, even stubbornness to stay away from accusing Grandma.

"Will any of these papers tell of the rumors about my grandmother?" I patted the stack and closed my eyes.

"No. Doubt the papers ever heard that rumor." Stasia pushed herself out of the chair. "We got to do something with this old man's clothes and stuff. Tell Bobby to haul in the boxes."

Working late into the evening, we cleared the house, stacking Old Joe's material life into the rear of a pickup truck used mostly for shot deer and strings of catfish. We marked some boxes Salvation Army, others personal, and still others trash. We left the bedstead, mattresses, and other heavy stuff. Bobby had a cousin who cleared out old things and would pick it up free.

"Now, Mae," he said as we stopped at a smelly trash pile and dumped some of the boxes. "What you planning to do with that little house?" He lifted a box and heaved it atop some mildewed tarps and plastic bags filled with household garbage. "I'll bet I know somebody who'd buy it from you, and the land. It'd make a great hunter's cabin."

I glanced at Stasia who rested in the cab. She fanned bugs away from her face. In the twilight, she looked old and tired. I shuddered.

"I'll probably live in it."

XIV

"Little Miss Alligator saw that old bull the other day. He weren't in no good shape, either." Grandma had drunk one whole Mason jar and started on her second. But today she didn't drift off. The amber liquid agitated her. She leaned forward in the rocker, planting her feet solid on the floor boards. She had slipped off her ragged shoes and scraped her toes back and forth along the wood. Her rocking, unrhythmic, sounded anxious.

"Old gator's tail nearly rotted off from some injury. Little Miss hung around the shore, hiding in the cypress knees where if he saw her he couldn't get at her." She shook her head furiously. *"Nope, he never saw her. Couldn't. His eyes had glazed over like them boiled fishes. Old Bull wasn't going to ever see anything again. Little Miss stayed all day near the giant cypress, then crawled on shore when the big moon came out. She stood there and watched Old Bull's boiled eyes drift down deep in the water and never come up again."* Grandma took a long swig on the jar, then leaned her head way back in the rocker. I stood, scared she would tilt over and break something.

"She's free of him, Mae. Won't never again that Old Bull hurt anymore gators." I stared. Grandma was laughing out loud. She toasted the moon, then saw me staring at her. *"Come here, child."* I moved closer, slowly, afraid of the flashing eyes and whiskey breath. *"You got to drink a toast to Little Miss Alligator. She done you some good."* Grandma grabbed my dress and

yanked me between her knees. She caressed my hair, then pulled my head back. Lifting the Mason jar to my mouth, she said, "Drink, child. Sip just a little for Little Miss Alligator." I squeezed my eyes shut, the preacher's sermon on the evil of drink running through my head like Satan after guilt, and let the liquid touch my lips. Grandma tipped the jar and I would have to drink or let it spill on my dress. The fury I expected from her overruled any fear I had of going to hell for drinking liquor. I sipped. A gasoline taste filled my head and nearly burst my sinuses. I swallowed, then stepped back and gulped air. "Good girl!" Grandma rocked back, the chair keeping rhythm again, and drank her own toast.

"I think those stories stopped that night," I said to Stasia.

We sat on her porch, neither able to sleep. "It was pretty much like tonight, full moon and clear."

"She wanted the best for you, Mae, wanted to protect you from some of the evils she knew about." Stasia sighed. "Did a damn good job of it, too."

"Couldn't she have been just a bit more, well, loving?"

"No, Mae, she couldn't. It wasn't her way. She'd never got that from nobody else. She didn't know much how to give it. Your Uncle Nast, now he's a good man, but he don't know how, either." She reached to me and pressed my arm with a chubby palm. "She loved with a fierceness all the same. I know."

We stood on the Bay Bridge—Stasia, Bobby, Aunt Becky and Uncle Nast, the preacher, and a few swamp people. Skipper Lou stood at one end in the shadow of an oak. I held Old Joe in my hands, ready to heave him into the river, a deep spot where the waters of the manatee and catfish mixed above deep limestone caves. "Say your thing, preacher," I said and held the metal box of ashes toward him. He prayed Old Joe's soul into heavenly peace, then nodded. In the still, humid sunshine of noontime, I opened the box. The gray ashes poured in a stream, straight into the river. When they stopped, I flung the box after them. It sank, chasing Old Joe to his eternal hiding place.

I rested an hour at Aunt Becky's house, then, with the bundle of old newspapers tucked in a paper bag, I headed for my box apartment in Tallahassee. Two days later, anxiety returned.

"We got a missing persons inquiry going on, Mae. Toller Gruman's been gone too long, and his widow wants to sell off some stuff to make ends meet. Some people say they saw you on the river about the time he disappeared. We got to put your statement in the record." Bobby dropped his head, looking at me like he ought to be chastised just for asking.

"Yes," was all I said. We met downtown in a tiny cement room with vinyl chairs and a square table. Bobby sat with the detective, glancing at me nearly every second, like I might fall and he'd have to catch me.

"People at your grandma's funeral say Toller showed up there." It was a question, not a statement. The detective, a man with piercing blue eyes under sleepy lids, waited.

I nodded. "I didn't know him, and I didn't know his name was Toller until much later. At the church, they only called him a Gruman."

"Got any idea why he went to the funeral?"

I shook my head. "No one at the church seemed to know." The detective wrote in a small tablet, then checked another page, I figured, for the next question. "You see him on the river during the days you were there?" He shoved over a picture of a proud Toller, his belly shoving against a tight undershirt, beaming beside a gutted deer. He held his rifle in his other hand.

"Yes, I saw him and some other men at the old fish cleaning shack."

"You talk to them?"

"Never!" I opened my eyes wide at the very thought. "They were drinking. I didn't think it safe to approach them."

"How come you saw them there?"

"It had come up a bad thunderstorm, and I thought I might get out of the rain."

"You didn't, then?"

"I got pretty wet." I sat stiffly, refusing to allow my eyes to give out anymore information.

The detective nodded. "Better wet, than raped. But I guess you know that." He never looked at me. "You see him again?"

"I saw some women camping on the river. Spent the night with them. Then, I saw Anastasia Skourous and her family, some old man checking his bush hooks, and this homeless fellow who turned out to be someone I knew years ago."

The detective stayed silent as he wrote all this down. When he finished, he looked again at his question page. "Okay, that's about it. I didn't expect you'd know anything. Man like Toller Gruman got demons running after him. Bobby here will bring you a typed-up statement to sign. Right now, I got to talk to the widow."

I stepped into the hall. Three people sat in chairs lined against the wall. The woman, not nearly as old as me, stared with colorless eyes underscored with black bags. Her cheekbones would have looked classic on a magazine model. On her, they told of few meals outside of grits and homemade whiskey. Her frail body, clad in a tee-shirt top and torn stretch pants, seemed swallowed by the plastic contour of the chair. Two children nearing their teens sat on either side of her, their mouths dropped in the perpetual condition of the retarded. Blank eyes stared at us like we were ants removing ourselves from underground living quarters. The girl's eyes never found mine, never showed recognition of the oar that slammed up side her tormentor's head. The boy's beginnings of a beard left tufts sticking from his chin and jaws in odd places. His sallow skin resembled a mangy dog. The eyes stared, like his sister's, uncomprehending. I waited for Bobby to escort them inside.

As they passed me, I smelled old grease and swampy mildew. And I heard the voices in my head. "I don't want to." And the incoherent beller of a girl in terror of knowing what was about to happen to her.

"You okay, Mae?" Bobby stood at the door, hesitating to go inside and leave me. "I'll be waiting for you to bring the statement."

I fled. The sheriff's department, my box apartment, the city.

"Ain't no reason for you to tell him about that episode with the boy," said Stasia. "You told him you saw the man, in the company of others. That's enough." She sighed. "Besides that boy has took enough. No need to embarrass him."

I left Stasia's place in my boat at twilight. My car, parked at Bay Bridge, waited at the roadside. So did Bobby.

"Hi, Mae." Bobby lowered his head and grinned. "Sheriff sent me out to ask another question. Hope you don't mind."

I shook my head and felt adrenalin shoot through my chest.

"Seems some fellow out here said you gave him a ride when he fell in the water. Is that true?"

I closed my eyes. Maybe Bobby sensed I was trying to remember. I hid relief. "Yes, there was this man. He came down from under the bridge there." I pointed to where the couple had gyrated in each other's arms. "I took him to one of the landings in the bay."

"Anything else you remember?"

I shook my head. "If there is, I'll call you." I watched Bobby's patrol car ease across the bridge and head back to the city. Overhead, clouds gathered and threatened the night. I slipped back into my boat and turned up the throttle. When darkness settled in, I turned on the boat light. Its beam cast around me, reflecting moss and cypress tree shadows off ebony waters. By the time I reached the old shed, rain beat steadily inside the boat. I tied up to the same tree branch and scrambled ashore. The rusting tin roof offered little protection from the wind that gathered about me, tossing sheets of rain from the open sides. I trekked through the forest without a light. At water's edge, I stopped and stared into the blackness. Rain and wind pelted me, like it wanted to push me away from the river. I stood firm, even though the rain turned to flood. "Come up, Toller Gruman!" I yelled. "Get out of that water and rise up here on shore where I can bash your head in good, then tell the sheriff about your nasty deeds. Get up!"

Loose mud toppled around my feet, and I sank up to my ankles. The storm gathered strength and pushed across the surface water, throwing the river against my shins. I stared, waiting for the moment when St. Margaret's would vomit up Toller Gruman's body right into my arms. When lightning came closer, its flashes lit up the bank like a torture chamber using electric shock. Once, when several flashes followed each other, I saw something move out of the bushes to my left. An alligator, maybe two feet long, but a baby nonetheless, slipped easily into the rushing river water. "Little Miss Alligator," I whispered to the elements, and my body eased. "Look after that Old Bull."

XV

Been pretty much listed as having drowned or maybe died out in the forest," said Bobby as he rocked on Stasia's porch.

"Ain't nobody really caring much. Toller Gruman was a mean bastard. Beat up near 'bout everybody he knew, including that old uncle of his."

"This marriage," said Stasia, "I don't think any of us ever heard he'd officially tied the knot."

"Did though," Bobby stopped to drink. He enjoyed being the one with the knowledge, the male in charge. "Found him this widow over near Apalachicola. She didn't have nothing except a boat her husband left her. Guess that's what Toller wanted. Sure didn't want them two half-witted kids she had."

I hung my head and stared into the marshy bank where a crop of cattails had shot up just inside the water. That's exactly what he wanted. I watched a river turtle poke his head out of the water. From a distance he looked like a snake, but he moved too slow, and after he neared the river bank, the outline of his shell appeared just below the surface. I watched him turn, find a rotten log and climb aboard. Pretty soon, three other turtles, not as big, joined him. "He didn't beat the kids?"

Stasia shot me a glance.

"Sure. Them and their mother. Woman stayed full of bruises. She sold off that boat and high-tailed it to Crestview or some place near there. Took them kids with her. Ain't nobody happier than her to see old Toller gone missing."

"How do you know he didn't go off somewhere by himself, that he won't turn up soon?" I felt my heart pounding, and stood to ease it. I rested my cheek against the wood support pole, its rough splinters digging into my skin.

"Didn't happen. His guns are all there, and his truck. Fishing gear. Nothing went with him. He's more likely dead. His old uncle said he'd been lifting the whiskey jar that day. Probably got off by the river and fell in, drowned. Could be he wandered into the swamp and fell in a sink, or just died somewhere and rotted in the humidity."

"Enough!" I said. "He's dead, then?"

"Can't be officially declared for a while, but I'd say yes." Stasia and I knew Bobby wouldn't come to this on his own, not out loud anyway. He had heard it from the sheriff.

"No Toller Gruman will litter this swamp another day," Stasia breathed heavily and stretched her legs. On her bare feet, especially around the ankles, blue veins met in a mass, giving the appearance of a night sky map I once saw in an astronomy book. "That's about the last of the Gruman's, too. His uncle still bush hooks around the river, but he ain't got no kids. Toller was the last of the line."

"The Old Bull." I closed my eyes and thought, Old Bull alligator with a rotting tail. Bobby looked at me and smiled. Calling Toller the Old Bull wouldn't mean much to him. He'd think I meant the sire of the family had died out, and I hoped he would think that. I met his eyes, sleepy dog eyes, faithful, protective. My heart skipped a little when I saw his future on my porch, his arms lifting heavy things to carry inside, his gun shooting the rattler that threatened my life.

"You planning on keeping Old Joe's property, Mae?" Stasia had stared at us a long time. A kind of knowing bounced between us.

"Plan to move in," I said. "A box apartment in the city isn't much of a place for a river girl."

Bobby sank into his rocker and swayed rhythmically, smiling the kind of contented smile I saw on Old Joe's snoring face when he sat in the porch swing.

I rest now, on the river. I drive into the city during weekdays and become another person for a few hours, but my home is here. I've redone some of Old Joe's place. The kitchen linoleum is new, the modern kind that looks more like tile. And the windows have white mini-blinds with yellow curtains. I had some people come out and fix the floors. Now they are shiny hardwood with woven Indian rugs. The Ageless Hippies like the look. They say the natural swamp light on the wood and Indian design brings back the days when the youth of America sat around on the floor, smoked joints, and contemplated their navels and the universe all night. They sent a green lava light and some incense for a house gift when I moved here.

Lillian Street and the others come by on Sundays every once in a while. They row their canoes to Old Joe's Landing—I put up a sign with that name on it. Then they trek up to the house on the narrow trail through the woods. I can hear them coming because they sing "Rollin' on the River" all the way to the edge of the yard. We mostly sit on the porch in good weather, singing sixties' songs and laughing till we have stomach aches. They still pass around a joint. One is usually their limit.

Bobby comes by and sits with me in a rocker until the light goes and we move inside. He keeps saying he's going to repair Old Joe's swing so we both can sit in it. I don't care much if he never does. It's a dying swing—the place where Old Joe died. I think about that night, maybe too much. I see Old Joe doing the clean-up with his functioning side, then darting off in the woods. He wouldn't have had time to make it back before the heavy rain started. When he got to his porch, he would have been drenched and nearly blinded by the downpour. His clothes soaked, his feet dragging through mud, he might have stumbled on the steps. When he finally got to the swing, his mind must have been racing over the deed, the second Gruman, and the second Pope woman. It just had to be too much to take. He rocked the swing, the rain blowing at him from the back, and heard the whispers of the swamp ghosts. Sometime in the night, he heard the right one and his brain just burst.

In my mind, I see him fall forward, maybe crying out for Grandma, landing on his face in a kneeling posture. Sometimes when the wind and rain howl through the trees around me, I hear the girl's voice holler for help and wonder if Toller is still there, but then I see Old Joe and know he's not. Sunday afternoons, I sit in the humidity until twilight. The misty swamp spirits visit my yard, steaming up through the spaces between the trees. They tell me the river has Old Joe and Grandma and Toller and Toller's daddy. They're all safe there at the bottom. My secrets are safe, too, here at the bottom of my jar. Bobby goes to sleep in his rocker long before dark.

Author - copyright © 1999 Melodie Earickson

A native-born Floridian, Glynn Marsh Alam was raised on a farm among the swamps and live oaks near Tallahassee, where she spent humid summers reading mysteries and swimming in creeks where alligators and snakes lurked in the foliage. She has been a decoder/translator for the National Security Agency, a university instructor and teaches English Literature now in Los Angeles.

Twice a year she journeys tback to North Florida to live among the critters, the moss, the deep, clear springs, where she calls upon eel grass and river currents to inspire sinister goings on in her stories. Glynn Marsh Alam has published two murder mystery novels, *Dive Deep and Deadly* and *DeepWater Death* and a number of short stories in literary magazines and anthologies.